# Riley Carson
## And The Cherokee Caves

### BY
## MEGAN WARGULA

Lisa,
Thank you
of me! En, ...
and always do good for
others!                  'es
                    Megan Wargula

## Cover Design by
## Andy Suggs and Megan Wargula

A portion of this book's profits will be donated
to animal welfare organizations.

D1329529

Copyright © 2016 by Hound and Thistle, LLC

Ordering Information:
Quantity sales. Special discounts are available on quantity purchases by corporations, associations, and others. For details, contact the publisher at the address above.
Edited by WT Editing

Printed in the United States of America

Publisher's Cataloging-in-Publication data
Wargula, Megan.
Riley Carson And The Cherokee Caves / Megan Wargula
p. cm.
ISBN 978-0-9973807-0-5
Library of Congress Control Number: TBD

First Edition

14 13 12 11 10 / 10 9 8 7 6 5 4 3 2 1

For Finlay & Riley, my muses.

For all the dogs I've loved and who have made an impression
on my heart and an impact in my life.

Thank you for your unconditional love.

xoxo

"The time is always right to do what is right."

-Martin Luther King, Jr.

# CONTENTS

# CHAPTER ONE

## *The Saddest Day*

Riley Carson pedaled her bike furiously as fear and worry swirled through her head. She had just gotten a message from her mom, *Head straight home, Sammy's not doing well.*

Sammy was the family's Yorkshire terrier and he had been battling cancer for months. Even though he was the family's dog, the bond between Riley and Sammy was like no other in the Carson household, they were deeply connected. Riley squeezed her stinging eyes tightly, her lower lip trembled.

Riley's best friend, Finn Murphy, looked like a cyclist trying to cross a finish line as he pedaled standing up and wobbled from side to side in an effort to catch up to Riley. As they rounded the corner and turned onto their street, he said, "Ri, are you okay?" Riley had shown Finn the text message before she raced toward home and he knew she was scared.

"I don't know, I just wanna get home. I have to get to Sammy." Riley tried to catch her breath in the thick, humid air and sweat ran down the middle of her back. She turned up her driveway and jumped off her bike with Finn at her heels. She looked at him with worry written all over her face, her large blue eyes searching his face, but for what, she didn't know.

"Do you want me to come in with you?" Finn was breathless as well, he wiped his face with the sleeve of his t-shirt, and pushed his sandy blond hair off his forehead.

"No, thanks…I just gotta go see him." Her voice caught and her eyes welled up with tears.

"Okay, call me later." Finn watched Riley turn and head to her house, he felt useless because he knew there was nothing he could do to help. As he hopped on his bike and headed toward his house, he thought about how much Riley loved her dog and knew that this was heartbreaking for her.

Riley ran up the wooden front porch steps and flung open the front door. "Mom, Dad!" She headed toward the kitchen where she saw her older sister, Hailey, listening intently to their dad. By the look on her dad's face, Riley knew this wasn't good.

Riley was frantic. "Where is he?" She felt fear and anxiety well up inside her, she felt like she was going to burst with emotion. "Is he okay? Daddy, please tell me he's going to be okay!"

Riley's dad, Jack, put an arm around her shoulder and said, "Come here, he's in the sun room."

Riley eased into the sun room with her dad, looking for Sammy. He was lying on a pile of blankets in a beam of sunlight with her mom, Priscilla, sitting with him.

"Hey buddy," Riley said as she walked over to him. Her mom got up from the little dog's side so Riley could be with him.

Sammy didn't move a muscle. Instead of greeting his favorite human with kisses and tail wags, Sammy couldn't even lift his head. Riley moved closer, maybe he hadn't heard her, "Sammy?"

"Dad, he's not acting right. He's not responding to me." Riley now searched her dad's face for answers, reassurance, something. Riley knelt down next to her little buddy and nervously tucked her brown hair behind her ear.

"Sam? Sammy? I love you." Riley looked at her parents and

said, "He's breathing, but something's wrong."

From across the room, Jack looked at his wife and whispered, "I think we need to make the call. Dr. Morgan said she could come here if we needed her to."

It was plain to Riley's mom that the time had come to let Sammy go. She dabbed at a tear in her right eye, then walked over and knelt beside Riley, putting her hand on her daughter's back. She knew Sammy would find comfort in Riley's arms. "Why don't you hold him and cover him with his favorite blanket, that will keep him warm and he's always so comfortable in your arms."

Riley gently picked up her sweet boy, laying him on her chest as she sat in the nearby chair. Her mom grabbed the warm alpaca blanket, Sammy's favorite, and covered them up.

Riley's parents and sister were in the kitchen while Riley laid with Sammy. She stroked his head and said, "I love you, you are the best dog ever."

Sammy began to pant, his warm, little head resting right over Riley's heart.

"I love you so much," she said, tears streaming down her cheeks and onto Sammy's soft, fine fur. "You're such a good boy. I love you."

At that moment, Sammy's mouth opened and he panted, slower this time. Riley felt something warm and wet on her lap. His panting had stopped. Her young brain was trying to process it. He lost control of his bladder. He had just died. Her beloved Sammy had just died while she was telling him how much she loved him.

"I think he died! I think he died! Mom, Dad!" Riley held on

to Sammy, still petting him, tears falling fast from her eyes, she was shaking as her family came into the room.

Her dad rushed to her side and said, "Here, let me take him."

"No!" Riley was wailing, red-faced, and devastated. She held Sammy to her chest, hugging her sweet boy. "No, he can't be dead, he can't!" She was scared to let him go. If she let him out of her arms, it meant he was really gone.

Riley's dad did all he knew to do. He gathered Riley in his arms and stroked her hair, gently rocking her as she cried into his shoulder. "Shh, shh, he's at peace now, he's not suffering anymore. He waited for you, Roo. He waited to see you before he let go."

Riley couldn't stop crying. She was hysterical, heart-broken. Her dad continued to hold her until finally she settled her breathing down and kissed Sammy on the head one last time. Riley handed her beloved dog over to her dad and curled up under Sammy's favorite blanket, crying out her pain.

### 

The night Sammy died was hardest on Riley. She cried all evening long, unable to deal with such a devastating loss. She was even too sad to eat and skipped dinner. Later that evening her dad came into her room with a cup of lavender and chamomile tea, hoping to help soothe her.

"Daddy, I'm never going to be able to love another dog again." Her face was red and tears streamed down her cheeks, Riley just couldn't stop crying.

Riley's dad set the tea cup down on her nightstand and sat on the edge of her bed. "You'll be able to love another dog again, sweetheart, it will just be a different love. No other dog will ever replace Sammy, but you have enough love in your heart to share with another dog. Tons." He smiled softly at his heart-broken daughter, he hoped talking about it would help her.

"Not yet, I don't. I…can't." Riley began to cry harder.

Her dad hugged her, stroked her hair and wiped tears off her cheeks. "Shh…it's okay, Roo."

After a few minutes, Riley took a sip of tea and settled her crying. "Dad, tell me the story about how I got my nickname again." She took the tissue her dad offered her and blew her nose.

Riley's dad loved to tell this story and was glad she wanted to hear it. He hoped it would settle her mind a bit. "Well, you were just a baby and you were in your bouncy-seat watching a nature show. You loved to watch anything with animals when you were a baby. This particular day you were watching kanga-roos bouncing across the Australian outback and you were just giggling like crazy."

Riley smiled at this and wiped her eyes. "I loved animals even as a baby?"

"You sure did. You were always a happy baby, but when you saw an animal, you got so excited." Her dad tucked her hair behind her ear, grateful to see a smile on her face. "You were bouncing and giggling at the kangaroos on TV and you said your first word, 'Roo'. It was the cutest thing. You started pointing at the TV saying, 'Roo! Roo!' just bouncing away. So, being that you were a bouncing little kangaroo yourself, you became our little Riley Roo." Her dad was smiling now, too.

"I like that story," Riley said, her eyes were getting heavy.

"I do too. Now you try to get some rest. I love you." Her dad gave her a kiss on her forehead.

"I love you, too, daddy."

# CHAPTER TWO

## The Found Dog

Riley spent Sunday resting and preparing to start middle school on Monday. She was really nervous about starting middle school but was relieved that she and Finn would have a couple of classes together, History and English. They also had lunch period together which made Riley really happy. She was shy and was relieved that she would have someone to sit with at lunch, not to mention her best friend.

Riley and Finn decided they would leave extra-early for school on Monday, something the ever-prepared Finn had suggested. They lived close enough to the school that they could walk or take the bus, and they decided to walk. Riley liked the freedom of walking to school and preferred the quiet walk to a smelly, crowded school bus. She was anxiously waiting for Finn on her front porch, her stomach already in knots.

"You ready?" Finn asked as he walked up the porch steps, a confident smile on his face, ready to take on this new adventure.

"Ready as I'll ever be." Riley drew in a deep breath.

Finn knew Riley was nervous about starting middle school. "It'll be okay." He gave her a reassuring grin. Finn seemed excited to start the day and see what kind of adventure it would bring, quite the opposite of how Riley felt at this moment.

"School just comes so easy for you. And now all the girls are so into what everyone is wearing, always trying to impress each other. It was so much easier when we were eight."

"Yeah, guys have it way easier. Sure there are cliques, but we don't worry about what other guys are wearing and stuff like that."

"I know. I'm not trying to impress anyone. I just want to be nice to people and have them be nice to me. And wear jeans and sneakers every day and not be judged for it." Riley looked at Finn and grinned.

Finn was happy to see Riley smiling. He knew Sammy's passing had devastated her, and while the two friends could talk about anything, he wasn't sure how to address it. Finn didn't want to upset Riley.

The two friends made it out of their neighborhood and headed down Mimosa Street toward the school which was still about five blocks away.

"I'm glad we have English and History together," Finn said as they passed the sprawling grounds of First Baptist Church of Roswell.

"Yeah, me too. I knew we wouldn't have math together, you might end up being my tutor."

"Yeah, and you can check all my grammar before I turn in any papers!"

"It's a deal!" Riley was so glad she had such a good friend in Finn.

"So, other than starting school, um, how are you doing?"

Riley knew he was talking about Sammy and felt her throat tighten. "Um, okay," she squeaked, trying not to start crying.

"Look, I'm sorry. I don't want to upset you, but it wouldn't be right if I didn't ask. Just know that if you want to talk about it, we can. I'm so sorry about Sammy, he was an awesome little guy."

Riley drew in a deep breath and managed to say, "I know you are. Thank you for asking, and for calling me yesterday. I just can't talk about it without getting upset. You know how it is."

"Yeah, I do." Something caught Finn's eye, "Hey, what's that?" He was pointing over at the bushes around the far left of the church.

There was something white moving in the bushes.

"Is it a dog?" Riley tried to get a better look as they headed toward the bushes to investigate. "Let's move slowly so we don't scare it."

"Good point. I'll go around to the left and flank it in case it runs when it sees you. Let's make sure it doesn't look rabid or anything. You never know."

As Riley approached she could tell it was a dog, but hardly recognizable as one. It was filthy, covered in mud as if it had been in the creek and its fur looked all matted. "Hey baby." She slowly crouched down, hoping not to scare the poor thing.

The dog immediately ducked back into the bushes.

"I think it's scared," Riley said. "I wonder how it got so dirty?" She took her backpack off and unzipped it. "Let's see what kind of food we have so we can lure it out." She opened her lunch bag and sorted through the mostly healthy food her mom packed for her. "Well, it's either my sandwich or an apple. Do you have anything better?"

"I have carrots!" Finn called out from the other side of the bushes.

"Your mom may be more of a health nut than mine! I'll try to give it some apple." Riley took a bite out of her apple to offer to the scared dog.

After about ten minutes of trying to get the dog out of the bushes, Riley and Finn realized this was not going to be easy, and they couldn't be late for school, especially on the first day.

"Let's call my mom," Finn said. Mrs. Murphy volunteered for a local rescue group and if they could catch her before she left for work, she would have time to get the dog and get it to them.

"Good idea. You call her and I'll see if I can at least snap a photo so we can make signs to post around the area."

With Finn on the phone with his mom, Riley pretended to ignore the dog so it would feel less threatened. She had to at least get a picture of it. After what seemed like forever, but was probably only two minutes, the little dog moved to an open space in the bushes and Riley took a couple of photos. She stood up and the dog darted back into the bushes.

"My mom will be here any minute, and she's called one of her friends at the rescue group who lives nearby so they can catch the dog. This looks like it could take a while."

"Yeah, and we need to think about leaving soon. I don't want to be late." Riley unconsciously touched her stomach, it always hurt when she was nervous and she hated that.

Mrs. Murphy got there quickly, after all, they weren't that far from home. She parked her SUV in a space on the street and headed over to the kids. "Thanks for calling me. You two still have plenty of time to get to school, but get going. I'll keep an eye on the dog until Rhonda gets here."

"It's right through there," Riley said, pointing to a little hole in the bushes. "Can you see its white fur?"

Mrs. Murphy squatted on the ground and tilted her head to look through the shadowy space in the bushes.

"Mom, it's pretty dirty. Looks like it may have been in a creek or something. It's covered in mud."

"Oh, yep, I see it," Finn's mom said, finally spotting a little of the dog's white fur in the back of the bushes. "It looks like it wedged itself up against the church. It's certainly scared. Alright, you two run along, I won't let this dog out of my sight."

"I hope we won't be late for school," Riley said, nervously twisting a strap on her backpack.

Mrs. Murphy looked at her watch. "Nope, you're fine. You two left so early, you still have fifteen minutes before the first bell and you'll be there in ten if you walk quickly. Just don't make any more stops." She smiled at them, her beautiful face was even prettier when she smiled, which seemed to be frequently.

"Thanks, mom! Text me when you catch it?"

"Will do! Have a great day at school you two!"

"Bye, thanks!" Riley said to Finn as they set off at a brisk pace, "I hope they catch it, poor thing looked terrified."

"I'm sure they will. Rhonda has been working in rescue for a long time, she'll be able to catch it."

Riley and Finn made it to school in plenty of time before the first bell. Riley's nervous stomach was bothering her, she hoped the rest of the day would be drama-free, but she wasn't so sure. Starting middle school was daunting.

# CHAPTER THREE

# *No Good Deed Goes Unpunished*

At the end of her first day of middle school, Riley was exhausted and tried to remember which direction would take her to her locker. After she headed down the wrong hallway, she took out her map of the school and figured out where to go to get back toward the front of the building where her locker was located. She got there and pulled a slip of paper out of her pocket that had the combination on it. She opened her locker on the first try for the first time that day and grabbed most of her books. She couldn't believe how much homework they already had on the first day of school! Before closing her locker, she carefully pulled a picture out of a binder and taped it to the inside of the door; she hadn't had time to do it this morning. Now Sammy would be with her at school every day.

Riley and Finn decided to meet outside the front doors to walk home together; she was eager to get outside on this hot, sunny day to get some fresh air. As she got to the front doors, Riley didn't see Finn, but noticed a girl she had seen at lunch talking to Corey Thornton over by a cluster of pine trees. This piqued Riley's interest because Corey always meant trouble. Riley hadn't met the girl, but figured her name was Eve because it was beautifully written on her backpack in a silver marker. Riley and Finn went to elementary school with Corey, he lived nearby, and he had always been a bully. Corey was bigger than the rest of the kids their age, he was a bulky kid who always looked dirty even though he came from one of the most affluent families in Roswell. Corey's dad was Hadrian Thornton, III who worked at the same law firm as Riley's dad, but whose family had "old money" and deep roots in Roswell. This meant that Corey got away with a lot–it seemed even the teachers were afraid of him.

Riley pushed open one of the four doors across the front of the school and heard the girl yell, "Stop it!"

Riley rushed over to see what was going on, Eve had no idea who she was dealing with and Riley wanted to help. As she approached her classmates, Riley could see that Eve was crying and said, "Hey, what's going on?"

Eve flung out her arm and pointed her finger at the ground, her hand shaking. "He's hurting this poor stray cat!"

As Eve stepped aside, Riley saw that Corey was taunting a scrawny, pathetic looking young cat; he had it pinned to the ground and was throwing pop-its at it. The sharp, fire-cracker-type pop was terrifying the cat. The poor thing was struggling to get away from Corey's fat-fingered grasp, but the cat was too weak and Corey too strong and mean. Riley's blood was boiling, she could see why Eve was so upset.

Riley felt her heart race and was furious. "Corey, cut it out! Stop doing that!"

"What? I'm not hurting it. Look, it peed itself!" Corey laughed at the cat's fearful response to his cruel treatment.

Riley felt her cheeks get hot and her heart was pounding now. How could he do this to this poor cat? Without a second thought, Riley's sneaker made contact with Corey's ribs. It startled him and stung him just enough that his grip on the cat loosened and it scrambled up the closest tree. Riley's back was to the school and she never saw Finn coming out the front doors with Mrs. Finkelstein, one of the sixth-grade science teachers, trailing behind him.

Eve was still crying and Riley was yelling at Corey, oblivious to anything else and enraged at his behavior. "You're so mean! How could you do that?"

"Young lady?" Mrs. Finkelstein said as she and Finn approached Riley, Eve, and Corey. Riley didn't hear her and was still yelling at Corey, her hands clenched into fists at her side, her heart still racing.

"Young lady!" Riley looked up. She can't be talking to me, she thought.

"That is *not* lady-like behavior!" The old lady pointed a long, bony finger at her. "What is your name?"

"Um, me?" Riley asked as she looked at this lady with confusion.

"Yes, you, who else would I be talking to?"

Riley looked at the teacher who had a sharp, pointy nose upon which sat humongous glasses that gave her the appearance of an insect. I wonder if she can even see, Riley thought, then looked around and realized there was no one else out here, but her, Eve, and Corey.

"Riley Carson, ma'am." Riley's breath was quick, her heart still beating fast. She was so angry, her adrenaline was still pumping.

"Detention for you, Miss Carson," Mrs. Finkelstein said.

"But, I was trying to help-"

"No buts, Miss Carson. Do you want morning or afternoon detention?" Mrs. Finkelstein reached into the pocket of her well-worn cardigan for her pad and pen, and a crumpled up tissue trailed out and fell on the ground.

"But Mrs. Finkelstein!" Eve said. "Corey was-"

"I said 'no buts' Miss Rycroft. Do you want detention, too?" Mrs. Finkelstein glared at Eve.

"You don't understand," Eve said, "Corey was hurting that poor cat!"

"Cat? What cat? I saw Miss Carson kick Mister Thornton and that is not lady-like behavior. Miss Rycroft, I warned you, no buts. You will be joining Miss Carson in detention. Mister Thornton, get out of here or you will miss your bus." The crabby old teacher scribbled on her pad.

Corey grabbed his backpack and smirked at Riley and Finn as he sauntered away to catch the bus, escaping discipline yet again.

"Miss Carson, Miss Rycroft, detention for one week, starting tomorrow morning." Mrs. Finkelstein turned on her heel and headed back toward school, stopping briefly to crane her neck up at the trees to see if she could spot a cat.

"Riley, I'm so sorry," Finn said. "I saw you two out here with Corey and figured something must be up and Mrs. Finkelstein followed me right out. One of the kids who went to Persimmon Elementary told me to watch out for her. She taught fifth-grade there and is supposedly a busy-body who gets all the kids in trouble. I guess now we know who she is."

"Yeah," Eve said, "I have her for science, she's pretty old-fashioned."

"She must be old-fashioned if she thinks kicking a boy who's hurting a cat isn't 'lady-like' behavior. What is this, 1952?" Riley was still mad, even more so with the injustice of detention from a teacher with outdated views. She took a deep breath, "It's okay, Finn. She sounds like an old biddy who thinks girls should wear dresses and bows and not stand up for themselves or others. No one ever wants to punish Corey, and I guess she didn't see the poor cat run up this tree." Riley looked up into the trees for the cat, she hoped it would be okay.

"Sorry, and thank you." Eve kicked at a weed with her Doc Marten shoes, her curly brown hair fell into her copper eyes and she looked up at Riley and Finn, "I'm Eve Rycroft. I just moved here from Savannah."

"No good deed goes unpunished, right?" Riley said with a smile. "I'm Riley Carson, and this is my best friend, Finn Murphy."

"Nice to meet you. I guess I'll see you tomorrow morning." Eve grabbed her backpack and she, too, looked around for the cat that was nowhere to be found, before heading home.

Finn looked up in the trees. "If it makes you feel any better, I saw the cat run up this tree."

Riley smiled. "Thanks. That poor thing, Corey was being so mean and I just lost it."

"I would have, too! I wish I had been out here instead of you." Finn reached into a deep pocket of his cargo shorts, "Here, let's do some ghost hunting on the way home." He pulled out his EMF meter which detects energy that ghosts can use to manifest themselves.

"You're trying to get my mind off of Corey, huh?"

"I thought I'd try." Finn looked at Riley with a wry grin, his green eyes sparkling. "That and you know how I love ghost hunting. With as many ghosts as there are in this town, you'd think I'd catch a lot more evidence!"

Riley's mind was still on the altercation that had just taken place and the unfair Mrs. Finkelstein. "I can't believe she gave us detention for a whole week!" Riley fidgeted with the strap of her backpack. "My mom is not going to be happy. I read in the student handbook that parents have to check students in to detention."

"You actually read the student handbook?" Finn said as he watched the lights flicker green on his EMF meter. "Your mom really isn't going to be happy. She'll have to wake up earlier to get ready."

"I know. She has to look perfect all the time, even in the carpool line. She's going to be really irritated. And yes, I read the student handbook." The two friends burst out laughing.

"I almost forgot!" Finn put his EMF meter away and pulled out his phone. "Check it out, my mom sent me this picture of the dog from this morning. It's a girl, the vet says she's about seven years old."

"Oh good, they caught her!" Riley looked at the now clean and fluffy white dog. "She looks so good!"

"Hard to believe it's the same dog, huh?"

"Totally." Riley's mood was lighter now. "At least something good happened today. We should make signs to put up to see if we can find the owner."

The kids turned the corner and Finn pointed to a sign post and said, "Looks like they beat us to it."

"Your mom is the best!"

"You know how she is, she wants to save them all."

"I know, I wish we could."

"Well, we can try."

# CHAPTER FOUR

## Detention, A First

As expected, Riley's mom was not happy that her daughter got detention, worse, was that she had to get ready early to drive Riley to school and check her in herself. On the way to school the next morning, Priscilla Carson chastised her daughter, "I swear, Riley, why can't you be more like your sister?" They were stopped at a red light and Riley's mom kept messing with her blond hair, trying to add even more volume to it, then applied what seemed like her third application of lip gloss. "Hailey has never had detention."

Riley fiddled with the strap on her backpack, looping and un-looping it around her index finger. "Mom, neither have I. My grades might not be as good as Hailey's, but I don't get into trouble. Corey Thornton was tormenting a stray cat. What was I supposed to do?"

Riley's mom smacked her thoroughly glossed lips. "Well, if Corey Thornton *was* tormenting that cat, he'd be in detention too, now wouldn't he?" Her mom turned suddenly and looked at Riley with a twinkle in her eyes, "Do you have a crush on Corey, dear?"

Riley was disgusted. "Mom, *gross!* He's the last person on Earth I'd flirt with, and I wouldn't flirt by kicking him in the ribs! He hurt that cat and the cat ran up the tree before smelly, old Mrs. Finkelstein could see it. She's blind as a bat. She's that one you joked about with the thick glasses that make her eyes huge."

"Oh, yes, the one who wears those dreadful moth-eaten cardigans over her dresses? She does needs some fashion help. And you're right, the glasses are horrible. She could stand to have a makeover, for sure. However, if Corey had done something, she would have given him detention, too, now wouldn't she?"

Riley couldn't believe it. It was bad enough that Mrs. Finkelstein didn't believe her, now her own mom didn't believe her and thought she was flirting!

"Well, at least we don't have to wait in the carpool line since we had to get you here so early," Riley's mom said as they pulled into the school drop off area. "All those women who drop their kids off wearing sweats and not a stitch of makeup. I just don't get it." They pulled into a visitor parking spot as Riley's mom fluffed her hair one last time and checked herself in the mirror for the umpteenth time. "Let's go check you in, little one. I swear they make us do this to punish us as well. Let's let this be the last detention, okay sweetheart?"

"Mom, I didn't mean to-"

"I know honey, you were standing up for a cat." Her mom gave her a wink. "I didn't think you even liked cats."

"Mom, I'm not fibbing! I'm a dog lover, but what Corey was doing was so mean! I would've been mad if it were any animal!"

"Okay, okay, let's just get you inside and get checked in." She put her arm around Riley's shoulder, giving her a squeeze.

Riley thought dealing with her mom every morning might be worse than detention. Lucky me, she thought, we get to do this for the rest of the week.

As Riley and her mom entered the school office, Eve Rycroft was there with a policeman. Oh no, Riley thought, what now?

"Hey Riley," Eve said as she saw Riley and her mom enter the office.

"Hi Eve, everything okay?" Riley looked at the tall policeman who was talking to the administrator.

Upon hearing this, the policeman turned around and said, "This must be Riley Carson."

Oh, great, Riley thought. I have detention at a new school with kids who are bound to be much scarier than I went to elementary school with, now this? A police officer who knows my name and is in the office with Eve. This can't be good. She swallowed, her throat felt like a gobstopper candy was stuck in it, "Um, yes sir?"

The police officer came towards her and squatted down to her level. "Miss Carson, Eve told me what happened yesterday. I think what you did was very brave." Noticing Riley's relief and confusion, the officer pointed to his shirt. It read: "N. Rycroft." He extended his hand and smiled. "I'm Eve's dad."

Eve noticed Riley's confusion at her dad's fair complexion and blue-gray eyes, "I'm adopted."

"Oh, thank goodness, I mean, err...sorry...I just thought we were really in trouble!" Riley felt like an idiot. She didn't know why seeing a policeman immediately made her nervous. After all, she'd only kicked Corey.

"I think you mean, Officer Rycroft, honey," Riley's mom said as she held her hand out. "Priscilla Carson, pleasure to meet you."

"You can call me Mr. Rycroft, but actually it's Detective

Rycroft," Eve's dad said to Riley with a grin. "Nick, pleasure to meet you," he said to Riley's mom as he shook her hand. "Your daughter has already proved to be a brave girl, and I appreciate her coming to the aid of my Eve. We just moved here from Savannah and starting middle school is tough enough as it is. Right, Riley?"

"Yes, sir." Riley thought Mr. Rycroft seemed nice enough. He had close cropped hair like most police officers Riley had seen and he stood very straight. Riley noted that his posture was way better than hers and she immediately stood up straighter.

"Well, my little girl just loves animals," Riley's mom cooed as she stroked Riley's long hair. "And she felt so bad for that poor cat."

Wait, what? Riley thought, now she believes me?

Mr. Rycroft leaned in and spoke in a low voice, "It sounds like Mrs. Finkelstein might have had a little trouble seeing what was really going on."

"Yeah, and Corey never gets in trouble. He's a Thornton," Riley whispered back to Mr. Rycroft.

"Aw, I bet Mrs. F just didn't see that cat, Riley, but I think her punishment was a bit harsh. I'm waiting to speak with the principal."

"Wow, thanks Mr, Rycroft!" Riley hoped he could get their detention shortened. Her mom was signing her in on the clipboard the administrator handed her, then told the girls to report to room 304. Mr. Gunn's room. Oh, great, Riley thought, Mr. Gunn? Seriously?

Riley and Eve arrived at Mr. Gunn's room and tentatively entered. Mr. Gunn was a tall, lanky man who was wearing a seersucker suit which offset his rich, dark skin and made him look super-tall. When he stood up, he towered over the girls. Riley thought he might be 6'5 since he was definitely taller than her 6'2 dad.

"Well, well, well," Mr. Gunn said when he saw the girls walk into the room. "Look what the cat dragged in!"

The irony of the statement was not lost on the two girls as they looked at each other. At least he's smiling, Riley thought.

"Hello, sir, I'm Riley Carson and this is Eve Rycroft." Riley was still frozen in place in the middle of the room.

"Well come over here, you two, and sign on in. It looks like you are my first guests of the morning. Most of my visitors don't get here as early as you two."

Riley walked up and signed her name and saw about seven names in total on the list. Mr. Gunn must have noticed this. "Yeah, amazing how so many kids already have detention after the first day, isn't it?"

"Probably Mrs. Fink-" Riley caught herself.

"Mrs. Finkelstein? Is *that* who gave you two detention?" Mr. Gunn asked, his voice going up an octave or two.

"Yes," Eve said, "but we were only trying to save a cat."

"What?! A cat you say? Was this that stray that keeps hangin' out around the pines in front of school? That thing needs to find a home."

"Yes, sir." Eve sounded like she had lost her voice it was so quiet. "A boy was messing with the cat and we tried to stop him."

"And Mrs. Finkelstein gave *you two* detention?"

"She said she didn't see the cat," Riley said.

Mr. Gunn started laughing hard at this one. "She didn't see the cat! Oh, lord! She didn't *see* the cat!" He settled his laughter down and said, "sorry, here's the deal. I'm going to need you two to make sure the rest of my guests sign in and get here on time. If they don't get here in time, they don't sign in. Got it?"

Oh, great, Riley thought, these other kids are going to realize that we're goody-goodies, and to top it off we have to check them in? This is going to be fabulous.

"Oh, and here," Mr. Gunn pulled a spare chair up to his desk, "you two, sit at my desk."

And it just got worse, Riley thought as the girls exchanged a glance.

"I'll be back in a little while." Mr. Gunn headed toward the door with long, easy strides. "Remember, if they aren't here by six-thirty, then bye-bye birdie!" The genial man was laughing loudly as he headed into the hallway.

"He seems nice enough to be the disciplinarian slash vice principal," Eve said as she and Riley giggled at the exuberant character they had just met.

They sat behind Mr. Gunn's desk, as instructed. Riley tucked her hair behind her ear. "At least we're here together."

"Yeah, could you imagine if it was just one of us."

"What do you think these other kids did?" Riley ran her index finger down the list of offenders.

"I don't know, but look," Eve said, "we're not the only sixth-graders. There are five other kids. One sixth-grader and four eighth-graders. All boys."

"Well, at least Corey isn't here. I'm actually glad about that now." Riley scanned the names, she stopped at one she recognized. "Oh, the other sixth-grader lives in my neighborhood, Tim Harrington. He's nice, just gets himself into trouble a lot. It's like he can't avoid it, but he's always been nice to me, so that's good."

"I actually met him yesterday," Eve said. "I was sitting by myself in science class and he moved seats to sit with me. I guess he could tell I didn't know a soul. It was nice of him."

Thankfully, all five fellow truants arrived on time. Riley was so relieved that she didn't have to get anyone into trouble for not getting there by six-thirty. All of the boys who had detention looked like the type who would have detention. Whatever that meant. They seemed surprised to see two sixth-grade girls sitting at Mr. Gunn's desk. The eighth-graders seemed to know Mr. Gunn really well.

As he signed his name, Tim Harrington asked the girls, "Why are you two here? How did you get this job?" Since Tim grew up around the corner from Riley, he knew she wasn't a trouble-maker, quite the opposite.

Riley looked at Eve, not wanting to go into the whole cat story. She didn't think this was the crowd she wanted to tell about her empathy for animals. "Um...Mrs. Finkelstein-"

"Good old Edna, huh?" A boy from the back who signed in as Bobby Snyder, and who clearly had good hearing, piped up. "What in the world could she want with the two of you? You look like you wouldn't hurt a flea!"

Riley laughed nervously and thought, If he only knew.

Eve spoke up in rapid-fire, "Actually, we were trying to save a cat from being hurt by another kid. Mrs. Finkelstein didn't believe us. Riley kicked the boy. Mrs. Finkelstein saw the kick, but not the cat. I was trying to explain to Mrs. Finkelstein what happened…she didn't want to hear it-" Eve was so nervous and practically out of breath.

"Wait, who was hurting a cat?" The boy with the sleepy eyes, long wavy hair, and a soft voice who signed in as Marley Phillips asked.

"Corey Thornton," Riley said the boy's name as if it tasted like sour milk.

"That's not cool," Marley said. "Is it the black cat with three white paws that hangs out in the pine area out front?"

"Yep, that's the one," Riley said, wondering how everyone knew about this cat except Mrs. Finkelstein.

"Really not cool," Tim said as he plopped into an empty desk in the middle of the room, "and Corey is nothing but trouble."

Riley thought Tim's comment was funny considering he was the one in detention and not Corey, but he was absolutely right. While trouble just seemed to find Tim, he was a nice boy. Corey, on the other hand, was just downright mean.

The boys all started talking to each other. It seemed like they knew each other fairly well. After about ten minutes, the speaker in the room crackled. "Y'all can get on outta there now. Miss Carson, Miss Rycroft, bring the attendance sheet to the office, please."

"Hey, must be start of the year generosity!" Bobby said. "Let's go!"

"I think it's because these two are here," Tim said, nodding at Riley and Eve. "Mr. Gunn seems like a good guy. He probably knows these two shouldn't be here."

Riley and Eve looked at each other with glee and Riley said, "Let's go to the office, then!"

# CHAPTER FIVE

## Mrs. Willnow

When Riley and Eve got to the office, their joy was short-lived as they saw the stern-faced librarian, Mrs. Willnow waiting for them. Mrs. Willnow was imposing considering her average height, probably because she had a sharp booming voice which was ironic for a woman who ran the quietest place in the school. She had an olive complexion with cropped light brown hair, light blue eyes and a look that could make a grown man shake in his boots. "I'll take that." She looked at Riley, extending her hand, waiting for the attendance sheet. "Let's see, Bobby Snyder, Marley Phillips…" Mrs. Willnow scanned the list, reading some of the names aloud. "The usual suspects. Then there's you two." She looked up from the attendance sheet at the girls and handed the paper over to the receptionist. "Put this in Mr. Gunn's box, please." She turned back to Riley and Eve. "Come with me."

Riley looked at Eve and mouthed, "What now?"

Eve shrugged, her pretty face washed over with worry. The girls followed Mrs. Willnow like little ducklings, down the hallway to the library. Riley was starting to get a stomach ache, her darn nervous stomach.

Mrs. Willnow opened the door to the library and let the girls in, following behind them. Since it was early, the library was fairly empty, yet Mrs. Willnow led the girls over to her office. She went around to her desk and the girls followed into the room behind her. "Close the door." Riley who was the last one in, closed the wooden door behind her, her stomach was twisting and turning. Riley and Eve sat down, unsure of what kind of trouble they were in now.

"Listen," Mrs. Willnow said, "Mr. Gunn told me about your detention and we both agree, it's ridiculous!"

Riley and Eve looked at each other, trying to figure out what was going on.

"Everyone in this town thinks the Thorntons should get special treatment because of their history here. Not me. I play by the rules. I honestly think Mrs. Finkelstein didn't see the cat, the poor woman can't see much, but I also know that Corey is a little trouble-maker. His reputation precedes him. Now, if you two said he was messing with that cat, I'm prone to believe you and I can't stand anyone hurting animals. It's just that when a teacher gives detention, we can't take it back. Mr. Gunn and I don't feel that the detention room is where you two should be for the whole week. And a whole week of detention was a little harsh."

"I agree," Riley said without even thinking. She looked up at Mrs. Willnow with a look of fear in her eyes.

"Smart girl." Mrs. Willnow grinned and her eyes twinkled. "So, Mr. Gunn and I decided that you two should work with me in the library for the rest of the week. Since it's the beginning of school, I have some things you can help me with, and if I run out of things, there's a whole library's worth of books for you to explore. Sound good?"

"Yes, ma'am," Eve said quietly, still sitting stiff as a statue.

"Sounds great!" Riley was totally relieved. She loved to read and even if she didn't get a chance to read any of the books in the library, she was starting to like Mrs. Willnow and always loved the peace and quiet of a library and the smell of old books. "Thank you!" Her stomach was starting to feel better already.

"Eve," Mrs. Willnow said, "everything, okay?"

Eve finally exhaled. "Yes, ma'am. I'm not used to getting in trouble."

Mrs. Willnow smiled. "Yes, it's good not to make a habit of it. Besides, you're new here and we can't have you making friends with the regulars in detention, now can we?"

Eve smiled and said, "Those boys were actually nice to us, thank goodness."

"Yeah, much nicer than Corey Thornton," Riley said.

Mrs. Willnow suppressed a grin. "Okay, it's almost time for first bell, so I'll see you tomorrow morning. Have a good day and go learn something," she said with a wink.

### 

Riley was so happy when Friday arrived. The week had gone by surprisingly fast considering she and Eve had library duty every morning this week. They enjoyed helping Mrs. Willnow organize the library and help put new books into the system. While Riley wouldn't miss having to wake up extra early for detention, she would kind of miss hanging out with Mrs. Willnow. She came across as being really strict, but she was actually a cool lady.

"Hi, girls," Mrs. Willnow said as Riley and Eve arrived for

their last day of detention.

"Hi, Mrs. Willnow!" They said, almost in unison.

"What can we help you with today?" Riley asked, eager to help.

"Let's see…We just received some donated books. Can you go through them and sort them based on type, then alphabetize by author, and make me a list? I'm running some updates on the computers, so just let me know if you have any questions."

"Sure, no problem," Eve said as the girls went around the counter to the boxes of books.

Riley started going through the books. "What if they are in pretty bad shape?" She held up a book that was very weathered, with loose, yellowed pages sticking out. She began to gently flip through it. "It looks really old." She noticed what look like handmade drawings as she flipped the pages.

Mrs. Willnow walked over and took a look at the book. "Oh yes, this was one of the books from a recent estate sale from a home in the Historic District. You'll probably find more like this, they are actually journals. You won't find an author, so just put them all together and I'll sort through them later."

"Okay." Riley stacked another journal on top of the one Mrs. Willnow had just set down. She peered into the box. "It looks like there's only a few anyway."

"Ooh, *Gone With The Wind!*" Eve pulled out the large tome from the same box. "I've seen the movie, but I've never read the book. I've always wanted to read it."

"Honey, you're just outside of Atlanta now, you better read the book or they might throw you out!" Mrs. Willnow joked, over her shoulder as she waited for another computer to update.

"We have several of those. You can borrow it, just bring it back when you're done and remind me that it was from the donated box. I doubt we'll have time to catalog it today." She was frustrated with the middle computer that was on the fritz again and was clicking the mouse repeatedly, as if that would help.

The girls went through all the books and soon had several stacks sorted by type, then alphabetized by the author's last name. There were lots of non-fiction books about history, presidents, the Civil War. Some classics like *To Kill a Mockingbird* and *The Catcher in the Rye* and the rest were an assortment of novels, then the stack of hard-cover journals. The girls showed Mrs. Willnow their organizational system.

"Looks good, girls. I think you've paid your debt to society," she said with a crooked smile.

"Thanks, Mrs. Willnow. It's been fun!" Riley said.

"Yeah, we'll have to come back to visit," Eve said.

"You better!" Mrs. Willnow had a great sense of humor and Riley loved how she joked with the girls. "Now just stay out of trouble."

"We promise!" Eve said as she headed to the door.

"You know us, we don't try to find trouble, it just seems to find us!" Riley said. "We're the good ones!"

Mrs. Willnow chuckled. "Have a good day. Now go learn something!"

### ###

The rest of the day flew by, and next thing she knew, Riley was meeting Finn at the front of school to walk home. "Mrs.

Willnow is really nice," she told Finn.

"Really?" Finn wasn't sure if Riley was joking or not.

"Yeah, really. She comes across all tough, but she's a cool lady. She's smart and funny."

"Kinda like someone else I know." Finn gave Riley a nudge with his elbow.

"Hailey is the one with all the smarts."

"She may be good in school, but she has no common sense. I think it skipped her and you ended up with it all. I secretly think that's why she's jealous of you," Finn said as he fiddled with his EMF meter, always trying to find evidence of ghosts in their town.

"Hailey, jealous? Of me? Ha! She's beautiful, smart, and popular. The last item being the most important to her and my mom." Riley kicked a small rock down the sidewalk with the toe of her well-worn sneaker.

"Yeah, well, you just have more discriminating taste when it comes to friends," Finn said with a smile. "Besides, you are street-smart and very wise. My mom always says you have an old soul."

"She's the best. I wish my mom would see me how yours does."

"Speaking of her, she has to run some errands tomorrow, do you want to come with us? I think she has to stop by the Angels Among Us adoption event at the Canton Street Antiques Market. Maybe there will be a dog for you and your family?" Finn hoped it wasn't too soon to mention Riley getting another dog.

Riley tucked her hair behind her ear. "I don't know if I'm

ready. My mom and dad seem really ready to get another dog, but I just don't think I can do it yet. Sammy was such an awesome dog, I'm just not going to love another dog the same way."

"I know, I think my dad feels the same way after losing Sadie, you'd think after almost a year he'd want to get another one."

"Yeah. I guess it does seem lonely without a dog in the house. Do you think your dad will want to get another one?"

"I know my mom won't have a house without a dog. She's threatened to keep one of our fosters, but they've all found homes pretty fast so she hasn't had to play that hand yet," Finn smiled. "But she will if she has to, you know how much my mom loves dogs."

"Yeah, about as much as I do!" Riley was smiling now. "I'd love to go with you and your mom." While Riley wasn't ready for another dog, she looked forward to petting dogs who needed love and attention. She hated that there were any homeless dogs.

# CHAPTER SIX

## *Meeting Molly*

Finn and his mom picked Riley up at noon on Saturday and they started off to run errands. Riley was excited to see the dogs up for adoption, even if she wasn't quite ready for another one. She was having a hard time dealing with Sammy's death and cried almost every day when she thought about him. Sometimes she swore she saw a small shadow come into her room, especially when she was at her drawing table, but she figured it was just her mind playing tricks on her. Wishful thinking, she supposed.

The first stop was the Angels Among Us adoption event because it was being held close by, in front of the Roswell Antiques Market. Historic Roswell's Canton Street had become a very popular place for people to shop and eat. There were lots of restaurants, some shops, and art galleries, all located along Canton Street in historic old buildings. Riley loved that they lived within walking distance of this area and her family often walked here to go to dinner, or in the warm months, to take part in Alive After Five when part of Canton Street was shut down. It seemed everyone in Roswell came to stroll, sample food from local restaurants, and listen to live music.

When they got to the adoption event, Finn and Riley helped Mrs. Murphy unload old towels and sheets along with toys and treats she had collected for the rescue group. Mrs. Murphy was great at getting donations for the group and was always asking for items that could help the dogs and their foster families.

Once they finished unloading all the donations, Finn asked, "Mom, can we go see the puppies?"

"Of course you can. I need to talk to Rhonda about a few things, I'll come get you when I'm done. Just make sure to stay out here with the dogs. And remember what I've taught you, don't reach over a dog's head to pet it, pet them on the chest." Finn's mom ruffled her son's sandy-blond hair.

"Cool! Thanks, mom!" Finn called over his shoulder as he and Riley headed over to a pen that had five puppies playing and rolling around.

Standing along the sidewalk were lots of foster parents and volunteers holding leashes for dogs up for adoption. While Riley loved seeing the dogs, especially the puppies, it made her sad that there were so many homeless animals.

"How could there be so many unwanted dogs?" She asked Finn, "How do we put a stop to this?"

Finn knelt and petted the puppies who had soft black fur and even softer pink bellies. Some of them liked to play tug with a toy, others wanted to be petted, while still others kept trying to nibble with their sharp little teeth. "I don't know. I guess we just educate people. Not everyone has a mom like mine who knows all this stuff. Take these puppies, as cute as they are, there are probably thousands more like them across the country. If people would spay and neuter, there wouldn't be so many unwanted litters."

As if the puppies knew what he meant, one nipped him on the wrist. "Ouch, that hurt!" Finn laughed, "Sorry buddy, I wasn't talking about your litter."

As Finn played with the puppies, Riley heard a slight whimper behind her. She turned around and a shy German Shepherd bowed her head and looked away.

"Hey there," Riley said in a high, sweet voice.

The dog looked back at Riley and inched closer to her.

"It's okay, I'm not going to hurt you." Riley extended her hand so the dog could smell her and make its own determination if she was to be trusted. She learned from Finn's mom that she should always let a dog smell her and to ask permission from the owner before petting an unknown dog. She could hear Mrs. Murphy's voice in her head, *Many dogs in rescue don't know the feeling of a kind touch from humans, we must show them they can trust us.* These words had stuck with Riley because they broke her heart.

Riley looked away since she knew direct eye-contact could be stressful to a dog, especially a timid one, her hand out-stretched so the dog could smell her if it wanted to. Then she felt it. First it was the weight of the dog's paw on her hand, then it was the jolt. It felt like electricity had just run through her body, though not painful, but a strong, jarring sensation, her body tingling. Then she saw the images.

Riley saw snapshots, a man wearing a baseball cap with a liquor bottle in his hand, hitting and kicking a cowering puppy, then tossing it outside. The dog, a bit older with a different family, seemingly a good one. Then there was a baby in the family, then this dog in a cold cement room, sitting in a corner, shivering, sad, heart-broken, defeated, facing the corner. Riley's stomach turned, simultaneously distraught about what she saw happen to this dog, and freaked out about what she just experienced. Can she feel what this dog feels? Can she see what happened to this dog? How was this possible? She had been around dogs all her life and this certainly had never happened before.

Immediately, Riley wanted to take this dog home, to finally give it the life it deserved, but she knew she couldn't. She was just a kid, and her mom would never want a big dog like this. This beautiful dog just wouldn't be the right dog for their family.

As Riley's head was spinning with thoughts about what had happened, Mrs. Murphy walked up. "Hi there, sweet girl," she said to the German Shepherd who was now politely sitting a foot from Riley. Kate Murphy slowly held out her hand which the shepherd promptly licked. "Oh, you really are sweet!" Mrs. Murphy knelt and scratched the dog on its chest which it seemed to enjoy.

"Mrs. Murphy," Riley said, "this dog has had a rough time. She was abused when she was a pup, then her next family gave her up when they had a baby-"

"That's right. How did you know?" The volunteer holding the leash asked.

"Oh, um, I-" Riley didn't know how to explain what she'd just rattled off and felt so stupid for blurting that out.

"They gave her up?" Mrs. Murphy interrupted. "After they had a baby?"

The volunteer was a woman in her late 40's who was short and stocky. She looked really strong, in an athletic way. She had close-cropped brown hair and was wearing high-waisted jeans and an Angels Among Us t-shirt with a sticker tag that read, *Deborah*. "I'm afraid so," Deborah replied, giving Riley a quizzical glance.

Mrs. Murphy wasn't happy. "Why do people think they can just get rid of their dog when they have a baby? Don't they realize their dog can be trained? Don't they realize that a pet is for life? Who makes the commitment to get a dog and just gives it up when a baby comes along?" She paused then said, "I'm sorry, I just don't get it and it makes me so mad. Pets are not disposable."

"Don't worry, ma'am, you're preaching to the choir," Deborah said. "We see it more than we like. This is Molly. She was abused by her first owner and when they tossed her out of the house, a concerned neighbor took her to the county animal control. Since she was still a pup and a purebred, she was adopted pretty quickly. The family who adopted her from the county shelter gave her a great life for a couple years, then they had a baby...I guess Molly here didn't fit into their lifestyle anymore and she was taken back to the county shelter who called us to help."

"They took her *back* to the shelter?" Mrs. Murphy was more riled up than Riley had ever seen. "I wonder if they knew that owner surrenders usually get put down first? They could have at least had the decency to try to find her a home."

"I know, it's awful," Deborah said. "Luckily, we have good relationships with many local shelters and this one called us right away. They knew we'd be able to find her a home. Molly's a great dog, though she's stuck in boarding because she had some aggression issues at her foster home. She's choosy about the men in her life, so we've got her working with a male vet tech who is training her." Deborah stroked the top of Molly's head.

"It's so sad." Riley tentatively reached to scratch Molly on her chest. She felt the soft fur of Molly's chest and waited. Nothing. Riley exhaled, relieved that she didn't have the same over-powering sensation she had when she first touched Molly. "No fun living in jail waiting for a home, huh, girl?" Molly seemed to confirm this by licking Riley on the tip of her nose.

"She's a beautiful dog. I'm sure she'll find a good forever home." Finn's mom had a wistful look in her eyes. "Are you two ready?" She looked at Finn and Riley.

"Mom, why don't we adopt Molly!" Finn was now petting the sweet dog who seemed to like him very much.

Mrs. Murphy looked at Molly, clearly wanting to take this sweet dog home with them. "Oh, Finn, I just don't know. I'm not sure your dad is ready for another dog…but she is pretty special."

"Well, we can always ask. Dad can say 'no' and we can convince him otherwise!" Finn was now sporting a cute devilish grin, his eyes pleading for his mom to consider this.

"Maybe we'll try." Mrs. Murphy now had a twinkle in her eye. "It's been nearly a year. He might be ready." She turned to Deborah, "Here's my card. If anyone else is interested, will you please let me know?"

"Of course," Deborah took the business card then looked at Finn and said, "Do your best!"

Finn hopped up. "I will, trust me, I will!"

Mrs. Murphy, Finn, and Riley headed off to run their errands. Finn was eagerly discussing his plan to convince his dad to agree to adopt Molly, but Riley was only half listening. Why had she felt Molly's experiences? It was so weird, it was like she could see a choppy film of Molly's life, at least the important parts of her life. Riley had been a dog lover all her life and had come in contact with so many dogs. Why this dog? Why now? Could she just be imagining things? Riley decided to put it out of her mind for now since there wasn't anything she could do about it. It was the weirdest sensation and it kind of freaked her out.

### 

After running errands, they headed back to the Murphy home. As they were unloading the car, Finn asked his mom, "Can Riley stay for dinner? Maybe she can help us convince dad to get Molly."

"Of course she can, but not because we want her to help us convince your dad, Finn." Mrs. Murphy ruffled Finn's hair. "Riley, why don't you call your mom and see if it's okay."

"I'm sure it will be. I'll give her a call." The Murphy's home was like Riley's second home and since Finn was an only child, it wasn't like they had a full house. She fit in so well with them, especially Mrs. Murphy, she often felt like she had more in common with her than her own mom.

Riley dialed her mom's cell number. "Hi mom, I'm over at the Murphy's house..."

"Oh dear, I forgot you were out! You went out with Finn, right?"

Really? My mom forgot I wasn't home? Am I really that invisible to her? "Yeah, we were running errands with Mrs. Murphy. They've invited me to stay for dinner, is that okay?"

Riley turned her back to Mrs. Murphy and Finn, her mom's words still stinging.

"Dear, I swear you practically live over there! I hope you aren't an imposition. Yes, it actually works just fine because your dad is working late on that big case, I've got Bunco tonight and I'm still getting ready for it, and Hailey, you know Hailey, she's such a social butterfly, she has plans to go to the movies. You'd just be bored here anyway, it's probably best that you stay with the Murphys."

While Riley was happy she could have dinner with the Murphys, she felt that familiar pang of hurt at her mom's words. Everyone at her home had something to do, and none of it included her. She was beginning to feel like an after-thought.

"Did your mom say it's okay?" Finn asked with a hopeful grin as Riley hung up the phone.

"Yeah, it's fine." Riley smiled and tried to hide the hurt in her eyes. Mrs. Murphy was cutting broccoli for dinner and gave Riley a kind smile. "My dad is working on this big case, mom has Bunco tonight, and you know Hailey," Riley often turned to humor to hide her pain. She flipped her hair in mock-super-model style. "Hailey is such a social butterfly, she has plans with her friends. Fabulous Hailey and her fabulous friends!"

All three of them started laughing as Mr. Murphy walked in the door. "What's so funny?" He asked as he walked over to his wife, put his arm around her waist, dipped her back, and gave her a sweet kiss.

"Mike!" Mrs. Murphy said as she swatted at him with a spatula. "You're a little stinky!"

Riley smiled at Finn's parents. You had to love them, because they loved each other so much and had a lot fun together. She wondered why her parents didn't act that way around each other. She knew they loved each other, but they seemed more stressed than fun and happy like the Murphys.

"How was the fishing today?" Mrs. Murphy asked.

"Pretty good. We had a good group today, I swear it's true what they say about beginner's luck. This corporate executive who never so much as dipped his toe in the water caught a trout this big!" He held his hands almost ten inches apart.

As Finn and his dad talked about fishing, Riley tuned out. She was thinking about what happened with Molly at the adoption event. She loved dogs more than anyone she knew. Why this dog? Why now? Would it happen again? She had to tell Finn, he always knew the answers, but she wasn't sure anyone could explain this. It would have to wait, it was almost time for dinner, and Riley knew Finn was going to start his lobbying to adopt Molly and she really wanted to help. Molly was indeed a special dog, whether or not one could "see" what had happened to her. Riley knew the Murphys would be a great family for Molly, a family that could give Molly the happy, safe life she so deserved for the rest of her life. Let Operation Adopt Molly begin!

Finn and Riley helped set the table for dinner while Mrs. Murphy pulled a baked chicken and sweet potatoes out of the oven and Mr. Murphy was upstairs showering.

"Okay, mom, we need to plan our attack. How are we going to get dad to agree to adopt Molly?"

"Now Finn, your dad is a reasonable man, we don't have to 'plan an attack', let's just ask him."

"But Mom, I'm afraid he's never going to want another dog

after losing Sadie. And I miss having a dog." Finn wore a sad expression that Riley didn't often see on his face.

"Honey, I know, I miss having a dog too, but no one should be convinced to get a dog and this is a family decision, so let's talk about it together. We'll just ask him."

"Ask me what?" Mr. Murphy was in the doorway with a big smile on his face. He was a tall man, built strong with broad shoulders. Riley always thought he looked like a lumberjack because he often wore plaid shirts when he wasn't working. He had changed into a t-shirt and a clean pair of jeans and smelled like soap. Much better than the fish he smelled like when he came home.

"Finn, go ahead and ask your dad." Finn's mom put a pad of butter on top of the steamed broccoli. "Riley, will you set this on the table?"

"Well, dad. We dropped some supplies off at the adoption event at the Antiques Market and there was this dog…"

"Oh yeah, what kind?"

Finn seemed to be stunned by his dad's response, because Riley knew that for the longest time Mr. Murphy didn't even want to discuss getting a dog. Kind of how she felt now that Sammy was gone.

"Um, a German Shepherd. Female. About 3 years old." Finn was trying to get all the details out as fast as possible before his dad could say no. Mr. Murphy had always had hunting dogs, either spaniels or Labradors, so they weren't even sure what he'd think of a German Shepherd.

"A German Shepherd, huh?" Mr. Murphy carried a bowl of salad to the table. "What's her temperament like?" He asked, looking at his wife.

Mrs. Murphy told her husband Molly's story which he too, got worked up about. This was definitely a family that knew a pet was for life.

"She's in boarding now." Riley piped up. "Stuck in a cage while they work on her training, or until she gets adopted. She's really pretty and since she's a purebred German Shepherd, she'll probably go fast." Riley hoped this would help Mr. Murphy make the decision they all hoped for.

All three sets of eyes were on Mr. Murphy who was looking out the window into the large fenced backyard that had been a playground for dogs they had loved and was now noticeably empty. He turned around and laughed. "Wow, why do you all look so serious?"

"Dad, if you could just meet her! She's a great dog, there's something about her. We know we can give her a home for the rest of her life." Finn was practically begging now.

"You know we could, Mike. She's had a rough go of it." Mrs. Murphy walked over to her husband. "She deserves a family who will make her part of the family. Forever."

Mr. Murphy put his arm around his wife's waist and looked at Riley, "What do you think Riley?"

"I think she's pretty special. There's…there's just something about her."

"Well, when can I meet her?" Mr. Murphy's eyes now back on his wife.

Everyone was smiling now. "I'll contact the rescue group and set something up. Maybe we can visit her tomorrow where she's being boarded." Mrs. Murphy gave her husband a kiss, then headed for her cell phone to text Rhonda.

"Awesome! Thanks, Dad!" Finn ran over to his dad and gave him a big hug.

"I think you're really going to like her," Riley said, smiling from ear to ear.

Mrs. Murphy put her phone down. "Okay, we'll see what Rhonda says. Now, let's eat!"

Mrs. Murphy's phone buzzed on the counter a short while later. Normally she would ignore it, but not tonight. If it was Rhonda, she wanted to answer it.

"It's Rhonda!" Mrs. Murphy said as she held up crossed fingers and answered her phone. "Hey Rhonda, how are you?" After a little chit-chat between the two, Mrs. Murphy's voice got serious. "Oh, okay. I see. Yes, Mike really wants to meet her. When is the other family coming to meet her?"

Riley's heart sank, and she knew her best friend's did as well. There were plenty of dogs to adopt, but Riley knew this one was special, not just because of what she felt when the dog touched her, but there was something intangible with this dog. Something that made Riley really want the Murphys to adopt her.

"Okay. We'll fill out the application. Alright, see you at noon." Mrs. Murphy hung up the phone, now she was the one who had three sets of eyes on her.

"Someone else is interested?" Finn asked with sadness clear in his voice. The wind had been taken out of his sails with that one phone call.

"Yes, but the group knows me very well, so that gives us a good shot. We're going to meet Rhonda at the boarding facility tomorrow at noon and they'll let each family meet and interact with the dog, review the applications, and determine which family would be best for her. Don't worry, whatever's meant to be will be."

"That's right. If both families are qualified to adopt, it sounds like Molly will get to pick and if we're right for her, she'll pick us. Now, I don't want you fretting over it, think positively." Mr. Murphy speared a piece of broccoli with his fork. "Let's enjoy this great meal your mom cooked before it gets cold!"

Riley said a quick prayer that Molly would pick Finn's family. She felt that Mr. and Mrs. Murphy were right, that thinking positively about it was the best plan. "How many dogs do you think they have at the boarding facility?" Riley asked Finn's mom.

"Gosh, I don't know. I think they board dogs at several places around the area, often it's veterinarian's offices that volunteer to board some of the dogs that need a little more assistance before they can be fostered or adopted. Why do you ask?"

"Well, I thought if I could convince my dad to take a break from work…maybe we could come with you to see if there are any other dogs that need to be adopted. I mean, my mom won't want a big dog, but we could check."

"I think that's a great idea!" Finn said, hopeful that Riley's broken heart might be on the mend.

# CHAPTER SEVEN

# Molly's Big Day

When Riley's dad heard her ask to go to the boarding facility to look for a dog, he was elated! Typically the Carsons would contact a breeder for a dog, but what the heck, they could at least see what kind of dogs were in need of homes.

Riley and her dad rode with the Murphys to the boarding facility and were discussing the adoption process. Riley's dad said, "Is it common to find purebred dogs through rescue groups?"

"You'd be surprised." Finn's mom said, "there are so many purebred dogs that end up in shelters. I know Priscilla is more accustomed to small dogs like Yorkies, so if we don't find one through Angels Among Us, you should check with the Yorkshire Terrier breed rescue group."

"Huh, I didn't realize they had those," Riley's dad said. "We just always went through a breeder."

"If you find a reputable breeder and want a puppy, there's nothing wrong with that, but adopting would be my first suggestion. There are so many dogs that need homes and breed rescues work with good breeders to find homes for dogs that end up in need," Mrs. Murphy said.

"What do you mean by a good breeder?" Riley's dad asked.

"All breeders definitely aren't created equally. Good breeders aren't in it for the money, they are champions of their breed and wish to produce healthy dogs that meet the breed standard. The dogs are impeccably cared for and a good breeder will even take one of their dogs back at any time in the dog's life and re-home it if a family can no longer care for their dog. The other types of breeders are what's called backyard breeders or puppy mills, people who don't really know what they are doing and are just in it to make a buck. There is so much that goes in to breeding a healthy dog, and the true, reputable breeders know how to do it well and want only the best for their dogs."

"But with all the dogs that need homes, isn't it better if we adopt one who needs us?" Riley asked.

"In my opinion, yes," Mrs. Murphy said as she turned around and smiled at Riley, "but I think there is a place for good breeders and understand if you want a puppy whose history you know."

"All right, here we are." Mr. Murphy pulled into the parking lot of the vet's office that volunteered to board some of the dogs that Angels Among Us couldn't place in a foster home.

"Angels Among Us is mostly volunteer-based and they don't have an actual facility. In order to pull dogs from shelters, they need a commitment from someone willing to foster the dog until adopted, or to rely on vets like this to board the dogs who have issues that need to be worked out before fostering or adopting out," Mrs. Murphy said to Riley's dad as they got out of the SUV.

"Wow, it's sad that there are so many dogs who need homes," Riley's dad said. "What a great group for doing all of this."

"Yeah, I follow them online, you wouldn't believe the stories some of these dogs have. It's really sad what humans do to them," Riley said.

Jack Carson looked at his daughter with pride. He was glad she was so informed on this issue, she clearly had a passion for dogs, more than he even realized. She had told him that she never felt as smart as Hailey, but he knew his youngest daughter had such depth and intelligence in a way that Hailey didn't. He wished she realized that book smarts weren't the only smarts one could have. "Well, then it's a good thing we're here."

An SUV pulled up and Rhonda got out. She waved at them with a smile. "I've got good news. The other family talked about it and decided they wanted a puppy so they are going to adopt one of the lab mix puppies!"

"Oh, that's great!" Mrs. Murphy said.

"Awesome!" Finn said as he looked at his dad.

"Well, if Molly likes us, so far it looks like I'm out-numbered," Mr. Murphy said with a wink.

"Rhonda, this is Jack Carson, and you know his daughter Riley," Mrs. Murphy said as Riley's dad extended his hand to Rhonda.

"Pleasure to meet you," Rhonda said to Riley's dad, then turned to Riley. "Thanks for all your help the other morning trying to catch the little white dog. Mrs. Murphy and I couldn't have done it with out you and Finn."

"Of course! Finn and I couldn't just leave it there. Is the dog okay?"

Rhonda glanced at Finn's mom and stiffened, "Yes, she's fine. She was hungry and needed a bath really badly, but we've got her in good hands. Okay, let's go on in." She led the families up the walkway to the side door. "The vet's not open on

Sundays, but since they board dogs, there's always a vet tech here. They are very accommodating when we have a potential family for a dog. Not only are they happy to help for the dog, but it frees up space."

The vet tech was a cute boy named Kevin who was in his early 20's with blond hair. Riley thought he looked like he could be on TV. Rhonda said that Kevin was in college to be a veterinarian and worked here on weekends. Kevin took the group to the back of the building into a room where there were cages on two walls facing each other.

"These are our clients' dogs who stay with us after surgery or when their families go out of town," he said motioning to the dogs on the right wall. "And these are our Angels dogs," he said pointing to the much fuller wall of cages on the left side of the room. "They are all up for adoption, or at the least, in need of a foster home."

"Wow, that's a lot of dogs," Riley's dad said.

"Yes sir," Kevin said. "It's a shame, isn't it?"

"Unfortunately, we've had an increase in stray dogs recently," Rhonda said. "It's odd, because most of them are smaller, pure-bred dogs that aren't in really good condition. They don't appear to be family dogs."

"Why do you think this is happening?" Riley's dad asked.

"Who knows, could be a hoarder, backyard breeder, dogs that were dumped. None are spayed or neutered so that makes it worse. They are out on the streets adding more dogs to the system. We spay or neuter all dogs that come to us, that way we can do our part in cutting down on unwanted litters."

"There's Molly!" Finn said, as he pointed to one of the large cages on the bottom row.

"You're here to see Molly?" Kevin asked. "She's a good girl. I've been working with her to help her get over her fears." Kevin walked over to Molly's cage, opened it, and took a treat out of his pocket before sliding a slip leash over her head. "She's gotten to know me, so she trusts me. We have noticed that she doesn't like baseball caps. She will growl and cower if anyone around her has one on."

Riley shuddered. The image of the man who hurt Molly when she was a pup…he was wearing a baseball cap. How in the world did she know this, see this?

Molly came out of the cage and her tail was wagging slowly as Finn knelt down. Molly must have known what was up, because she played her cards right, promptly giving Finn a big kiss on the cheek. Then she headed over to Mrs. Murphy. She was still wagging her tail and seemed so happy.

"Wow," Kevin said. "I haven't seen her this happy, ever! She really does seem to like you guys."

"I bet that's what you say to everyone," Mr. Murphy joked.

"Oh, no, I wouldn't do that. I know that finding the right home is what these dogs need. If they go home with the wrong family, they'll just be back here again. She seems really comfortable with you guys."

"Well, we met her yesterday," Mrs. Murphy said as she pointed to herself and Finn who were both now on the floor with Molly. "He's the deciding factor," she pointed to her husband.

As if she knew what Finn's mom had just said, Molly went over to Mr. Murphy and sat perfectly before him. Finn's dad squatted down and extended his hand to allow the pretty dog to get to know him by smelling him. Molly's nose was twitching and sniffing, then she moved closer to him, squeezing her large body in between his legs, rubbing her head on his knee.

"Well, I think she likes me!" Mr. Murphy had a wide smile on his face; he petted Molly and scratched behind her ears and just above her tail. The look on her face was as if she was in heaven.

Mrs. Murphy stood and crossed her arms over her chest. "Well, mister, what do you think?" She asked her husband as she grinned down at him. She loved that he looked like a kid, gleefully petting this sweet dog.

"How can I say no? She's such a love!"

The Murphys talked with Rhonda about the particulars. Their application had already been approved, it was just a formality since the organization knew the Murphy family through Kate's volunteer work. Finn sat on the cold floor, petting Molly who was soaking up the attention.

Riley and her dad were looking at all the dogs in the cages. "It's hard to believe there are so many up for adoption, huh Roo?"

"Yeah, Dad, and there are so many more. These are just the really unlucky ones that don't have a foster home." Riley stopped at a cage that housed one of the many pit bull mixes. "None of these look like dogs that mom would want, do they?"

"No, they don't. You know your mom, she wants a small dog that doesn't shed. I don't think these guys, as beautiful as they are, would be a good fit for our family." He patted Riley on the head.

"That's good, because I was thinking the same thing."

Riley's dad was surprised because he thought after seeing the Murphys adopt a dog, his daughter would want to do the same thing. "Really?"

"Really. These dogs will make great pets for the right family. If we find a dog that is right for us, that will open up another foster home and one of these guys can get out of here until they find a permanent home."

"That's very wise of you, Roo. Very responsible."

"Well, if more people were responsible when it came to their pets, we wouldn't have all these homeless animals. I'm very happy for Molly, and the Murphys. We'll get a dog when we're ready."

Riley's dad could still hear the reluctance in his daughter's voice. Sammy's loss still stung. "You're right, we will." He put his arm around her shoulder and gave her a reassuring squeeze. He understood, it was still too soon.

"You're all set!" Rhonda said to the Murphys. "Molly, you just won the lottery, my dear!"

"Rhonda, thanks for everything. Now you'll get to see Molly all the time!" Mrs. Murphy gave her friend a hug.

"Thanks, Kevin," Mr. Murphy said as he shook the vet tech's hand, "thanks for all you do here."

Riley and her dad told Rhonda what they were looking for in a dog and told her they would be in touch when they were ready.

It was a good day. The best day in the world for Molly, because she finally got the family she deserved.

# CHAPTER EIGHT

# *Cherokee Legend*

Riley's parents thought it would be nice to invite the Murphys and Rycrofts over for dinner, after all, the Rycrofts were new to the area and hardly knew anyone. A dinner party was set for the following Saturday.

"Riley, tell us about Eve's family." Riley's mom said as she cut fresh flowers for a vase in the foyer.

"Well, you've met her dad, he's with the Roswell Police Department. Eve's mom died, but I don't know how, and didn't ask because it didn't feel right. She has an older brother, Evan who is 16. I haven't met him yet, so I really don't know what he's like." Riley folded napkins for her mom. "She mentioned to us at school that day that she's adopted, but she hasn't talked about it."

Riley's mom arranged flowers into a large crystal vase. "Well, Detective Rycroft was so nice when we met him at the school, and with them being new to town, they probably don't know many people yet. I figured we should be hospitable and get to know them."

"Where's Dad?"

"Where do you think?" Her mom nodded toward the study. "Working. As usual."

"At least he doesn't have to work tonight."

Hailey walked into the kitchen and asked her mother, "Do

I *really* have to stay here for dinner tonight? I mean, it's Riley's friends coming over, not mine."

"Yes. We're having a family dinner with other families." Their mom was now cleaning up the clippings from her flowers. "You are part of our family and you will join us. Honey, how would it look if you weren't here?"

"But mom, I have better things to do." Hailey always had a way of saying things like this as if she were better than everyone in the world.

"Hailey, I know you have lots of things you'd prefer to do, but this is one night. It's not going to kill you to have dinner with your family on a Saturday night. It's a cookout and we're eating early, so if you want to go out with your friends after dinner, you may."

"Good. No offense, Riley, but you and your friends are just kids and I'm in high school." Hailey sauntered past Riley and into the sun room.

Riley's mom looked at her younger daughter and gave her a sympathetic smile. "Honey, you'll understand when you're older. Even though you two are just a few years apart, it can seem like ten when you're the older sister."

"No problem." Riley tried to shrug off the hurt she felt. She had always yearned for her sister to actually like her, but that didn't seem like it would happen any time soon, if ever.

Riley helped her mom get ready for their guests. She placed tea lights in mason jars outside on the patio, set-out pretty pink and black paper plates and napkins, and cut lemon slices for the sweet tea.

Riley's mom fixed her famous potato salad and dumped a

large can of baked beans into a pot on the stove. "There. All we need is your dad to fire up the grill and we'll be good to go."

Just then, Riley's dad walked in and over to his wife. "Ready for me yet?"

"Just about. We still have time before you need to start the grill." Riley's mom turned to her, "Honey, I know there wasn't a dog for us at the boarding facility, but how about we check out Perfectly Posh Pets? Hailey and I have stopped by a few times and played with this adorable Yorkie..."

Riley's dad looked at her with worry.

"Mom! That's a pet store! Those dogs come from puppy mills!"

"Oh honey, those puppies need good homes, too."

"Mom, do you know what happens to the parents of those dogs? They are kept in awful conditions, they don't get enough food or medical attention and they are stuck in cages their whole lives. It's horrible!"

"Well," her mom said as she stirred the baked beans, "the puppy we've been visiting seems perfectly healthy."

"He may or may not be," Riley was on the verge of tears, her voice raised and quivering, "but pet store puppies come from puppy mills and the parents are so mistreated. You shouldn't even buy a can of food or toy from those stores! We can't support those people."

"Okay, okay. We understand, Roo," her dad said as he came over to give his daughter a hug. "We will not buy a dog, or anything else from a pet store." He looked at Riley's mom when he said this, giving her a look that he meant what he said, and that they should change the subject.

"Riley, I didn't mean to upset you, honey. It's just that I miss having a dog so much and thought we might get that little fella I saw at the store."

"I'm sorry, Mom, I didn't mean to raise my voice." She went over and hugged her mom. "Those dogs are just treated so bad. We can't support that."

"Okay, I understand." Her mom hugged her back and then held her shoulders at arm's length, looking into Riley's big blue eyes, "I didn't realize where those puppies come from, and if it's as bad as you say it is, we won't shop at a pet store."

"Thanks, Mom. Maybe Rhonda will find us a dog, or maybe you can check with the Yorkshire Terrier Club of America to see if they have one up for adoption? Mrs. Murphy said that every breed group has a rescue, so we can rescue a purebred dog if you want."

"I think that's a great idea!" Riley's mom kissed her on the forehead. "Now, no more stress, our guests will be here soon!"

### 

When the Rycrofts arrived, Riley was taken aback at how cute Eve's brother was. He was tall, slim, and had kind eyes that sometimes hid behind his longish hair. He looked a bit like Mr. Rycroft, but a little mysterious. Riley thought he looked like a movie star, the quiet, brooding type who could just as easily play a pirate, or a poet. Just as she was introducing herself, Hailey walked in, appearing from out of nowhere it seemed.

"Hailey Carson," Hailey said as she put on her mega-watt smile and extended her hand. "I've seen you around school. I didn't know our *little* sisters were friends." She tossed her blond locks over her shoulder.

Evan smiled politely and said in a quiet voice, "It's nice to meet you. I've heard a lot about your little sister. She's been a good friend to Eve." He turned to Riley, "Nice to meet you."

"Nice to meet you, too," Riley said. He seemed like a nice guy and he just complimented Riley in front of Hailey which made Riley proud.

"Riley, did you hear about what happened with Tyler Harrison?" Eve asked, referring to the heart-throb singer who every young girl had a crush on.

"No, what?!"

"He got in trouble for gambling on greyhound racing."

"Big deal." Hailey rolled her eyes. "I don't even think that's illegal. At least he wasn't driving drunk again."

"It's illegal in the state of Georgia, where he was caught, and in most states," Mr. Rycroft said. "There are only a handful of states that actually allow it anymore."

"Oh." Hailey was not accustomed to being corrected and was a little irritated about it.

"And it's cruel," Riley said.

"Yeah, it's an awful sport, if you can call it that," Mrs. Murphy said with a clear tone of disgust.

"That kid seems to be in trouble all the time," Riley's dad said.

"But he's so cute!" Eve said.

"Was," Riley said, mad that the young heart-throb was into greyhound racing. "Those greyhounds are kept in cages all the time, only let out to race for human entertainment. I won't listen to his songs anymore."

"Cute will only get him so far," Mr. Rycroft said to his daughter.

"I know, dad," Eve said. "Don't worry, we won't do any of the stupid things he does. He's just cute and his music is so good."

This time it was Evan who rolled his eyes. "You call that good? It's so over-processed, I don't even think he *can* sing!"

"I know, I know. You don't think it's *real* music." Eve smiled at her brother. Clearly these two had this debate before.

"I'm with Evan," Finn said. "That's not real music. He could learn a thing or two from The Beatles."

"That's my boy!" Mr. Murphy said patting his son on the back.

"It's like no one actually sings anymore." Finn said.

"Yeah, it's not about the music anymore, it's about the per-formance and making money." Evan said.

"Well, *I* like his music." Eve wasn't going to back down.

"It's all a matter of taste; we can settle this over burgers," Riley's dad told everyone. "Come on, let's go out on the patio and enjoy this beautiful evening."

It was indeed a beautiful late summer evening in Georgia. The citronella candles were burning to keep the mosquitoes at bay which was customary in Georgia in the summer. The fami-lies had a really nice dinner, sharing stories and getting to know one another better. Even Hailey stuck around the whole night, but Riley knew it wasn't because she wanted to hang out with the Murphys and Rycrofts. Hailey had her eye on Evan, who surprisingly didn't seem interested in her one bit. He was having a nice time talking fly-fishing with Mr. Murphy and talking to Finn about music. Riley was just glad to have her whole family together, along with old friends and new. This was the happiest she had been since Sammy died.

"So," Riley's mom said to Evan and Eve, "do you two like Roswell so far?"

"Yeah, it's a cool place," Evan said. "I like that there's a lot of history here, kind of like Savannah."

Eve shifted in her seat and looked a bit uncomfortable. "Yes, ma'am. It's a nice place. I'm just really glad to have made friends with Riley and Finn…"

"Some kids at school were telling me about the Cherokee Caves. Do y'all know anything about them?" Evan asked.

Hailey laughed, "That's just a legend, you don't really believe they exist do you?"

Riley was surprised that Hailey had just talked down to Evan since she seemed to be attracted to him. Hailey must have realized it too and tried to correct herself. "I mean, they're cool stories, but I don't think they're true. Dad, what do you think?"

"I don't know, Hailey, I heard the same stories growing up. Sometimes legends can be based on facts."

"What's the legend?" Finn asked.

"I heard that there are caves somewhere in Roswell that the Cherokee Indians used to hide their gold," Evan said. "And supposedly they are booby-trapped to keep anyone from getting the gold."

"Gold? Booby-traps?" Finn said, "Cool!"

"Is that true, Dad?" Riley asked.

"Yep, that's the legend."

"Have you kids learned about the Trail of Tears in history yet?" Mr. Murphy asked.

"Of course," Hailey said, "the Native Americans were sent West under the Indian Removal Act of 1830 signed by Andrew Jackson."

"Forced off their land," Evan said. "Our mom was part Cherokee, so I learned about this when I was a kid."

"Yes, and here in North Georgia, not only was the land prime for growing cotton, but gold had been discovered so the government really had an interest in this land," Mr. Murphy said.

"Some Cherokee stayed here and lived peacefully with the settlers, so the legend said that the Cherokee who stayed hid their gold in caves around the Chattahoochee River," Riley's dad said.

"Wow, has anyone found it?" Finn asked.

"Well, if they did, they didn't let anyone know about it," Riley's dad said. "But I imagine if they really did hide gold around here, it would be long gone by now."

"Do you know where the caves are, Dad?" Riley asked.

"No, my buddies and I looked for them when we were about your age, but we never did find them."

"It would be so cool to find them!" Finn said.

"I just think it's a legend," Hailey said. "Surely if they existed, we'd know about them by now."

Finn who was not to be deterred by Hailey's opinion said, "You never know! The Cherokee would definitely pick a place that would be hard to find. The caves might just be sitting, waiting to be found!"

# CHAPTER NINE

## *Exploring Old Mill Park*

It had been about a month since the Murphys adopted Molly and she had settled into life with the family perfectly. Finn and Riley took advantage of a warm late September Saturday to take Molly over to Old Mill Park which Vickery Creek ran through. Vickery Creek was not some little creek, it was a wide creek that flowed into the Chattahoochee River. Like the Chattahoochee, Vickery Creek had lots of large rocks underneath the water and the kids knew to be careful, only playing along the banks. After one of Georgia's heavy rains, the creek became very treacherous. Water that looked like chocolate milk flowed furiously after a rain.

"Hey, how about we try to do some ghost hunting around the mill ruins before we head to the creek?" Finn said as they headed down the steep path that led to the covered bridge and trail system.

"I'm always game for ghost hunting, hopefully it won't be too crowded, but it is such a pretty day." Riley followed Finn and Molly down the dirt path to the left.

"Yeah, I know. I read that some people have captured EVPs and want to see if we can, too." EVP stood for Electronic Voice Phenomena, voices that can be heard on a digital recording but not to the naked ear.

"That would be neat if we could!" Riley said as she, Finn,

and Molly headed toward the Mill ruins, all three of them walking at a brisk pace now.

"Isn't it cool that this was a textile mill and there are still pieces left here?" Finn said.

"Yeah, it's so sad about what happened during the Civil War, though. To know that the wives and children of the mill workers were shipped out of here during the war, after Sherman came through...it's awful."

"I know." Finn ducked under a low branch along the path. "Once the Union soldiers found out this mill made cotton for the Confederate soldiers, it was all over...even though they flew a French flag at the mill, trying to trick Sherman and his troops."

"You gotta figure with all the destruction and devastation that happened here, there must be some paranormal activity around the ruins," Riley said.

"That's what I'm thinking. It would be so cool if we capture something!"

As they headed down the wooden decking to the area where old, rusted machine parts lay like an industrial graveyard, Finn got out his EMF meter, scanning it around the ruins. At one point, the lights changed from green to red and Finn got all excited, his face lit up like the lights on his device. He pulled his mini digital recorder out of his pocket and said, "Let's do an EVP session."

"Okay." Riley waited for Finn to ask the first question. They had done this many times and she knew that he was anxious to start.

"Is there anyone here with us?" Finn asked as the two waited to give time for a response and Molly decided to sit down and sniff her surroundings.

After a long pause, Riley said, "Did you work here at the mill?"

Another long pause. "Were you a soldier in the Civil War?" Finn asked, checking the lights on his EMF meter which had gone back to green. "If you're here, can you make the lights on this turn red again." He held up his detector. They waited, but nothing happened.

"Do you have anything you want to tell us?" Riley asked just as a family came around the other side of the ruins.

"Look!" Finn pointed to his EMF meter which went from green to red, right back to green. The family had stopped to look around the ruins and a group of older teens approached. Finn said so only Riley could hear, "Let's go. We'll have to come back when it's not so crowded. Besides, it could have been a glitch, this thing is steady green now."

"Oh well, we tried," Riley said as she felt a chill run up her back. She looked around but saw nothing.

"Yeah, I'll listen to the recording when I get home and let you know. Let's head over to my fishing spot."

Riley, Finn, and Molly headed back toward the covered bridge so they could cross it and head to a less crowded spot of the creek. "Most people will be down by the waterfall near the ruins and right along the banks under the bridge," Finn said. "I don't know why no one goes to my spot, but I'm glad they don't, maybe I'll catch something!"

"It's definitely pretty by the waterfall, but probably not good for fishing," Riley said as she now had Molly's leash and was watching the ground, making sure there were no snakes around.

While Riley loved being outside, she didn't like snakes and knew they could easily come across one along the creek's banks.

"You're so funny," Finn said.

"Why?"

"You're always looking at the ground for snakes." Finn knew his friend all too well.

"Well, I don't want to step on one!" Riley wished she didn't think about snakes every time they were on the creek banks, but all it took was that one snake swimming in the creek to freak her out. It was bad enough she had seen a snake, worse, it was swimming! "Besides, a copperhead or water moccasin could really hurt us, or Molly," she said of the very poisonous snakes that were common in the area.

"We've never even seen those!" Finn said as he stopped at a point just before a bend in the creek. "We've seen garter snakes and king snakes, and they aren't poisonous."

"They're snakes! I still don't want to step on one, no matter what kind it is!" Riley really wished they were talking about something else, talking about it made her more uneasy. She was far from a girly-girl, but one thing she didn't like was snakes.

"They're more afraid of you than you are of them." Finn prepared his fly-fishing pole. "Besides, I'm sure Molly will alert us if one is around," he said with a wry grin.

Finn had been working on his fly casting skills and while he hadn't caught anything today, Riley could tell he was getting better at casting. "You're getting pretty good," she said as she and Molly sat perched on a large rock behind where Finn was fishing but far enough to his left that they were clear of his line. Riley had her legs pulled up to her chin and hoped the rock was large enough that a snake wouldn't slither up it. She also told herself that maybe Molly could actually warn her if a snake was around. Finn had said that snakes have an odor about them and with Molly's keen sense of smell, she hoped this was a possibility.

"Thanks. Not as good as my dad, though," Finn said as he worked the line.

"Well, your dad has been fly-fishing for a long time. I can tell you're getting better." No sooner had Riley said this than Finn caught his line on something behind him and to his right, in the water right near the bank.

"Shoot! See, not as good as my dad!" Finn said as the two friends laughed.

"Here, let me help." Riley and Molly hopped off the rock.

Finn was already following his line down to the sticky, muddy bank where a pile of leaves and debris from upstream had collected. Riley stood higher up the bank, and didn't want to get too close in case there was a snake in that large pile of muck. Finn tugged on his line but it wouldn't budge.

"What is this thing stuck on?" He asked as Molly whimpered.

Riley looked down at Molly. "It's okay," she said as she petted the top of Molly's head. "Can you tell what it's stuck on?"

Finn was now digging through the muck, trying to find the end of his line. "Almost," he said.

"I hope it's not a snake!" Riley was only half-joking.

"I wish it were." Finn's face grew serious. "It's white." He smoothed away a lot of mud and revealed a dog.

Riley gasped, "Oh no!" She put her hand up to her mouth. It took all the courage she could muster up, but she tentatively moved closer to Finn. "Is it…alive?"

"It looks like it hasn't been here long, but it's definitely dead and it doesn't look like it was treated well. It's so skinny."

Riley knelt down next to him, laying her hand on the small dog's side. She felt nothing and quickly pulled her hand away as Molly began to whimper again. "It looks like the dog we found."

"You're right," Finn said as Molly's whimper turned into a deep, low growl.

Riley and Finn turned around to see Corey Thornton and his dad, Hadrian, coming down the path with their fishing poles.

"Hey kids," Mr. Thornton said, then noticed the grim faces looking back at him. "Everything okay?"

"Searching for Confederate treasure?" Corey asked with a smirk.

"Not quite, Corey. We just found a dead animal," Riley said as she stood up. Molly was now pulling on the leash, still growling.

"Oh dear," Mr. Thornton said.

"What's wrong with your dumb dog?" Corey said with less bravado, he backed up and adjusted the brim of his baseball cap.

"Corey…," Mr. Thornton said with a slight air of disapproval. "Do you need our help?" He asked as Molly's growling continued.

"No, thanks," Finn said as he looked over at Molly. "We'll take care of it."

"Uh, okay, if you're sure…" Mr. Thornton looked over Finn's shoulder, trying to get a look at what they had found. It was too covered in mud and he was too far away to even make anything out. He certainly didn't want to deal with it and was happy to get out of there, glad that the kids hadn't accepted his offer for help. "Come on, Corey, let's go."

As the father and son headed past them and toward the covered bridge, Molly began to settle down. "Let's call Eve's dad." Riley pulled her phone out of her back pocket.

"Good idea. Do you think he's the right person to call?"

"Well, if not, he can tell us who we should call." Riley was really anxious and Mr. Rycroft was the adult they knew who lived closest to the park and he was a police detective after all.

Mr. Rycroft arrived within fifteen minutes. "Hey Finn, let's see what you two have found." He squatted down and pulled disposable gloves out of the small bag he brought with him. With a gloved hand, he gently wiped away more mud and debris from the small white form. "It's certainly a little dog, but it's hard to tell what happened here with all the water and mud. Could be that this little dog got lost and got caught up in the swift waters and drowned."

"There's no collar," Finn said, "and look how skinny it is."

"I'll take it to a vet and have it scanned for a microchip and maybe we can find the owner," Mr. Rycroft said, avoiding Finn's gaze. As he pulled out a small, thick bag, Riley turned away. She just couldn't watch this anymore. Mr. Rycroft gently placed the small, lifeless body into the bag and sealed it up.

"Thanks for coming out here," Finn said. "We just weren't sure what to do." He looked at Riley who was biting her lower lip, her arms folded across her chest.

"You did the right thing," Mr. Rycroft said as he stood up. "I'll take it from here. Thanks, kids."

"Mr. Rycroft?" Riley said, her brow furrowed.

"Yeah?"

"Um, well, you seem to think this dog got lost…but what if someone hurt it?" Riley was wondering if her imagination was getting the best of her.

"Well, it might be hard to tell since it's been in the water, but we'll have the vet do an exam. And like I said, if it has a microchip, we can contact the owners. Let's not worry until there's something to worry about, okay?"

"Okay. Thanks, Mr. Rycroft." Riley wasn't so sure she believed Mr. Rycroft. She felt a cold shiver again. Something wasn't right…something was nagging at her. This dog looked similar to the dog she and Finn found on the first day of school and she wasn't sure it was a coincidence. Although she didn't have a weird sensation when she touched it, Finn was right, the dog was pretty thin, she could feel that.

# CHAPTER TEN

## Riley's Gift

Finn called Riley after church on Sunday, "Hey, can I come over? I want to play you a recording from our EVP session."

"Did you find something?" Riley hopped off the barstool she was sitting at in the kitchen, listening intently into the phone.

"I think so…I want you to hear it!"

"Yeah, come on over!"

When Finn arrived at Riley's house minutes later, she was in a rocking chair on the front porch, eagerly awaiting his arrival. "Okay, I can't wait to hear this!"

Finn took out his mini recorder and a pair of headphones from his backpack. When Riley put the headphones on, Finn hit "play." He watched as Riley listened intently, she turned her head to the side and squinted her eyes, closing them briefly. Riley's eyes got big and she said, "Rewind it, I want to hear that again."

Finn reversed the recording, and pressed "play" again. Riley put her hands over the headphones, on top of her ears, she bowed her head as she listened. Finn's voice came on first, 'If you're here, can you make the lights on this turn red again.' Then there was a long pause and Riley heard her own voice say, 'Oh well, we tried.' In the split second after Riley said that and before Finn said, 'Yeah, I'll listen to the recording when I get home…' she had heard something. It was very faint, but there was another voice. She looked at Finn and said, "One more time."

Finn reversed the recording again and turned up the volume a couple levels, again Riley closed her eyes and bowed her head as she listened closely. After this third listen, her head popped up, her eyes wide. "Oh my goodness!"

"You heard it?" Finn said as Riley slipped off the headphones and handed them back to him. Her mouth had fallen open.

"Yeah, totally."

Finn pulled a small notebook out of his backpack and tore a sheet of paper out and handed it to Riley. "You know the drill."

Riley took the paper and a pen from Finn and wrote something down. She handed the pen back to Finn and folded her paper in half as he wrote something on a page in his pad. They never wanted to influence each other if they did hear something, so they agreed on this plan. Finn showed Riley what he had written and she said, "Yep," and unfolded her paper and showed it to him.

The two kids had both written: Be Careful

"Wow," Riley said, "what do you think it means?"

"I don't know, but this was the only EVP I got. It didn't answer any of our questions, just said those two words. It sounded like a man, but in a whisper."

"It did…that gave me the chills!" Riley said as she rubbed her hands up and down her arms.

"I know, I just don't know how to take it…it could mean anything. People were injured while working at the mill so it could be a residual haunting, something just left over from the past and on repeat…or it could be warning us about something, but what?" Finn was serious as he looked at Riley.

"Well, if it was just like, 'Hey, be careful there's a snake behind you,' I honestly don't think a spirit would use all its energy to warn us about something like that. I don't mean to get all crazy with my imagination, but this was shortly before we found that dog."

"It's so cool that we captured it, I just really don't know what to make of it," Finn said.

"Yeah, well, we'll just take his advice and be extra careful in general, I guess." Riley plopped back down into one of the rocking chairs. "So, there's something I need to tell you about."

Finn looked at Riley, "Everything okay?"

Riley drew in a deep breath, tucked her hair behind her ear, and exhaled. "Yeah, everything's fine, it's just…something weird happened and I've been trying to figure out how to tell you so you don't think I'm crazy."

Finn sat down on the rocking chair next to Riley and set his backpack at his feet. "What's up?"

"Well, when we went with your mom to the adoption event, when we met Molly, I had a strange experience."

"Okay…"

"When I touched Molly, I could *see* what she had gone through."

"See? What do you mean, *see* what she had gone through?"

"When I touched her, I felt a jolt of electricity and I could see things. I saw her get hit and kicked by a man outside a trailer. I saw love she received from a different family. I saw a baby in the new home, then I saw the new family leave her at a shelter. I saw her scared and alone, shivering with fear on a concrete floor in a shelter. I saw all of this like one of those really old black and white movies with no sound, just images. It was really fast, but I saw it."

Finn's mouth dropped open, his expression one of amazement. All he could say was, "Wow."

"But more than what I saw, was what I felt...I could feel the emotions she felt," Riley said. "That's how I knew Molly's story before the volunteer told it to us."

"Yeah, you did." Finn thought back to the day they met Molly at the adoption event. "I didn't even think about it then."

"You think I'm crazy, don't you?"

"No. I'm just...stunned. Why didn't you tell me before?"

"I honestly didn't know what to think, and I felt like it was crazy," Riley said.

"I don't think you're crazy...I'm just trying to figure it out."

"Me too. It's not like Molly was the first dog I ever touched. I've never experienced that before, and I haven't since."

Finn rested his chin in the palm of his hand and thought it over. "Have you touched any other animals since?" Then it dawned on him, "The dog at the creek. You touched it! That wasn't like you and I was surprised, but there was so much going on, I didn't think about it. Did you feel anything when you touched that dog?"

"No. In a way I was hoping I would, but there was nothing." Riley thought for a moment as she and Finn both got quiet. "Sammy. He died in my arms the day before school started. He was literally laying on my chest, his head on my heart, when he passed. Do you think that could be it?"

"The fact that he died in your arms says a lot. He trusted

you, he was comfortable with you…," Finn said. "You loved him so much, Ri. It's possible that your love, his dying in your arms, it's possible it changed something."

Riley was thinking it over, glad Finn didn't think she was nuts. Then it just dawned on her, "The cat."

"Huh?"

"The cat at school! I was so upset after having lost Sammy, and then seeing Corey hurt that cat made my blood boil. It got free because I kicked Corey and he lost his grip."

"You're right! Think about it Ri, first Sammy died, *in your arms*, then you saved a cat from being hurt. Maybe the combination of the two instances changed something for you. I mean, it's possible."

"I guess so, it's the only thing I can think of that makes some kind of sense."

"I bet that's it, just think of it as a gift."

"I don't like a gift that makes me see things that are tough to see," Riley said.

"Yeah, but you've been given this gift for a reason. Just think of it like a super power. You can use your gift to do good!" Finn said, trying to lighten the mood.

"Okay, but don't go making me wear a cape, because then I'll really get made fun of!" Riley felt better having told Finn about her "gift" but was still so confused by it. She had certainly touched Molly since the first time and didn't feel a thing. She thought to herself, Maybe I only feel something when the animal needs help?

# CHAPTER ELEVEN

## Eve's Story

At school on Monday, Finn and Riley found Eve at lunch time and grabbed a spot at the end of a table in the back corner of the busy lunchroom. As the trio opened their lunch bags and began eating, Riley said, "Eve, your dad was so nice to come help us at the park on Saturday."

"What do you mean? My dad didn't say anything…," Eve said as Riley and Finn exchanged confused looks.

"Your dad didn't tell you about Saturday?" Finn asked.

"No, what happened?"

Finn and Riley filled Eve in on what happened at Vickery Creek.

Eve gasped when she heard about the dog. "Oh no! Do you know what happened to it?"

"No," Finn said. "Your dad took the dog and was going to take it to the vet to see if it had a microchip. He thought maybe it was someone's dog that got lost and drowned."

"I don't know, though," Riley said. "I have this weird feeling. It looked a lot like the dog we found on the first day of school. It just seems weird."

"Well, my dad will sort it out." Eve was picking at her food now.

"Why do you think he didn't tell you?" Finn asked.

Eve looked at her new friends, they had already proved to

be good friends to her, but she wasn't sure how they would react to what she thought was the reason her dad didn't tell her about what they found Saturday.

Riley noticed the concern on Eve's face and said, "Is everything okay?"

"Yeah, it's just…weird." Eve shifted in her seat and looked down at the table.

"What's weird?" Finn asked.

"Well, you know I'm adopted. My parents were killed in a car accident when I was just a baby and my dad was the police officer on the scene. I was in the car, too."

Riley gasped, "Oh my gosh, Eve, I'm so sorry."

"Neither of my parents had much family to speak of, so the Rycrofts adopted me. I believe they were meant to be my new parents. Then when my second mom died, I started…seeing her again." Eve looked up at Riley and Finn and searched their faces for a reaction.

"Wow," Riley said just above a whisper.

Eve continued, "I had a really hard time, I missed my mom…and I just started seeing her."

Riley noticed the sadness in Eve's eyes and couldn't imagine going through so much at such a young age. She may not have a lot in common with her mom, but couldn't imagine losing her. She didn't know what to say.

"It's like she's with you, to make sure you're okay," Finn said.

"At first I thought it was my imagination. You know, like wishful thinking. I missed her, so I saw her, but then I began seeing other people. Dead people. There were lots of them in Savannah and it seems like there's lots of them here, too. My dad just worries about me and I think he just wants to protect me from it all. That's probably why he didn't tell me about the dog."

"I had no idea," Riley said thinking about her experiences with Molly. "Is it scary?"

"Sometimes…I don't see them all the time, which is good. I tend to see them when I'm sad or stressed. It would be okay if I just saw my mom, but it's only recently that I've started seeing other ghosts." She paused then exhaled. "So you guys don't think it's freaky that I can see ghosts?"

Just as those words came out of her mouth, Corey Thornton and his buddies were passing by their table. "Did you just say you saw ghosts?" Corey said to Eve as Brad and Seth snickered.

At that moment, Mrs. Willnow who had overheard part of the conversation walked up to the table and said, "Corey, don't be silly. Miss Rycroft is re-reading the classic Dickens tale, *A Christmas Carol.* You know the story, where Ebeneezer Scrooge is haunted by ghosts of Christmas past, present, and future? Have you read it, or just watched the cartoon?"

Eve wondered to herself if the whole school had heard, it wasn't like she was talking loudly about it. Her stomach churned. This was beginning to remind her of her old school in Savannah. She busied herself with tidying up her trash.

Corey turned around to find Mrs. Willnow eye to eye with him, a stern look on her face. "But she said she *sees* ghosts! And who reads Christmas books in September?"

"Some people really like Christmas, Mr. Thornton, I myself start decorating right after Halloween. This is precisely what happens when you eavesdrop on conversations in which you are not involved. You only heard part of the conversation where

Miss Rycroft was re-telling what Ebeneezer Scrooge experiences in the novel. Now, why don't you and your friends move along. If you're done with lunch and have nothing to do, you could always help me stack books in the library," Mrs. Willnow said with a grin.

"We were just leaving," Corey said, his Brad and Seth trailing behind him like ducklings.

Riley was amazed that Corey listened to anyone. He seemed almost scared of Mrs. Willnow. "Mrs. Willnow, that was great! I've never heard a teacher put Corey in his place like that. Aren't you worried he'll tell his dad and you'll get in trouble?"

"I'm a tough lady from Nebraska, I can handle the Thorntons."

"Thanks Mrs. Willnow. I really appreciate it," Eve said.

"No problem. Just be careful who's around when you're talking about...*books*," she said with a wink to Eve, then headed off to scold a kid who had just missed the trashcan and was content to leave his trash on the floor.

"Well, I can understand why your dad didn't tell you about what we found Saturday," Finn said. "It was tough to see. I don't even like thinking about it."

"Me neither," Riley said as she took another cookie out of a plastic baggie.

"So," Eve said, "you don't think I'm weird?"

"Of course not!" Riley was feeling kind of relieved that she knew Eve wouldn't think she was weird when she found out about what Riley could sense. "Besides, Finn is always trying to find ghosts. He's always trying to find evidence of the paranormal." Riley grinned, hoping she would make Eve feel better.

"I think ghosts are cool," Finn said. "There are so many stories around town about haunted places. Sometimes Riley and I go ghost hunting, but she's a little scared of some places we go to, like the Creepy House."

"What's the Creepy House?" Eve asked.

"It's that old gray house at the corner of Atlanta Street and Cedar Street. It's supposed to be haunted by a little girl and a really creepy man," Finn said.

"Yeah, I don't like to go near that place. It's super-creepy, I just get a weird vibe there." Riley said.

"We should tell her about the EVP!" Finn said.

"Oh my gosh, yes!" Riley sat up straight, her eyes bright with excitement.

"Remind me what EVP stands for?" Eve said.

"Electronic Voice Phenomena..." Finn began to explain as Riley interrupted.

"Recorded sounds that the naked ear can't hear, basically," Riley said, then looked at Finn and smiled. "Sorry."

Finn smiled back, "It's okay. So, we were at the mill ruins Saturday, by Vickery Creek."

"You know, in Old Mill Park not far from your house," Riley interrupted again as Eve nodded.

"So we went to the ruins and did an EVP session-," Finn said.

"But there were too many people, I mean it was a Saturday after all, so it was kinda busy," Riley said.

"Yeah, so we asked a few questions and my EMF meter lit up a bit," Finn said.

"Remind me what an EMF meter is?" Eve said.

Finn looked at Riley who said, "No, you go ahead," grinning and stifling a laugh.

"Electromagnetic field meter," Finn said. "They are used to measure fluctuations in magnetic fields because it's believed that ghosts can manipulate these fields."

"So the EMF meter flickered a couple times, so we asked some questions," Riley said.

"Yeah, like 'Did you work at the mill? Did you fight in the Civil War?', stuff like that," Finn said.

"Finn even asked, 'If you're here, can you make the lights on this turn red again.' But nothing happened."

Eve looked like she was watching a tennis match, as she looked back and forth from one eager friend to the other as they retold the story.

"Then Riley said, 'Oh well, we tried,' and before I shut the recorder off, the voice said in a whisper, 'Be careful.'"

"No way!" Eve said.

"I know, can you believe it?" Riley said.

"It's cool, but it's also kinda scary," Eve said.

"Yeah, we don't know what to make of it, but how cool that we actually got an EVP!" Finn said.

"People were starting to walk around the trail that weaves through the mill ruins, so since we didn't get anything from the EMF meter, we figured it wasn't an ideal day anyway. It's so neat that we actually did catch something!" Riley said.

"It's cool that you got evidence of it," Eve said. "I was so worried you'd think I was making things up. A lot of people don't believe in ghosts and if they do experience something, they usually try to explain it away. I mean, it is kinda weird."

"Well, they say we only use ten percent of our brains. I just think that means you use more than ten percent," Riley said with a kind smile.

The three kids finished up their lunch and got ready to go.

"Well, one thing's for sure, Mrs. Willnow is right," Finn said. "I think we should be careful when we talk about...*books*."

"I agree," Eve said.

"Yeah, me too," Riley said.

As Eve headed off to class, Riley grabbed Finn's arm. "Hey, do you think it's weird that Eve's dad didn't say anything to her about Saturday?"

"Well, he does seem protective of her, and with his job he probably has good reason to..." Finn said, "but it is kinda weird that he wouldn't mention a dead dog."

"Yeah, and the fact that he said it might be someone's pet that drowned...that just doesn't seem right." Riley thought for a moment. "And that dog looked so much like the dog we found at the church."

"I guess I didn't think about it that much, but it is weird. I think Mr. Rycroft is a good guy though, you don't think he's up to something do you?"

"No, well, I mean..." Riley didn't know what to think. "It's just nagging at me. I don't think that dog was someone's pet that drowned."

"Well, hopefully we can figure out what happened. Come on, or we're going to be late for class," Finn said.

# CHAPTER TWELVE

## *An Innocent Excursion*

Riley and Finn went to Sloan Street Park in Eve's neighborhood, not far from Vickery Creek, to hangout out with Eve after they finished their homework on Wednesday. Riley and Eve swung on the swings while Finn and Molly laid in the grass nearby.

Riley looked at Finn who was laying in the grass with Molly's head on his belly. "It's cute, you and Molly look like you're spelling something that begins with a 'T'."

Finn laughed, "Yeah, 'T' for trouble, that's us, Molly!"

"Yeah, right," Riley said as she pumped her legs and swung higher. "That dog hasn't been a bit of trouble. I can't believe her last family dumped her."

"I know, she's the best." Finn scratched Molly behind her ears; she yawned, licked her chops, then closed her eyes.

"Hey, what if you guys show me the place where you found the dog?" Eve asked as she slowed her swinging down.

"Yeah, sure," Finn said, "and have your dad kill us? I don't think so!"

"Yeah, I don't think that's such a good idea," Riley said.

"I just want to see if I can sense anything there. Wouldn't it be nice to see if we could find out more about the dog? I've been thinking about it non-stop since Monday."

Finn sat up, as did Molly, and said, "What do you think?"

Riley looked concerned. "I don't know. I don't want to get into trouble."

"We'll be quick, I promise. Don't you want to see if I can figure anything out?" Eve asked, trying to convince Riley.

"Okay, but we go to the spot, show you, then leave. If your dad finds out, we're all in trouble." Riley tucked her hair behind he ear, hopped off the swing, and headed across the green grass.

"I promise, he won't find out. He's working, he'll never know we dangerously went to the banks of the deadly Vickery Creek!" Eve joked as she giggled and got off her swing.

"Hey look, that swing is moving by itself," Riley said as the three of them looked at the swing set. "Neither of us were on that swing."

Eve looked back at the swing set, smiled and said, "Must be because we jostled the set when we got off. Come on, let's go before it gets dark."

The friends headed through the pretty neighborhood that was a mix of old homes that mill workers lived in, like Eve's, and newer homes that were built to look old. The newer homes had courtyards with pretty gates and low brick walls that Riley really liked. "One day I'll have a home with a courtyard like that, with lots of flowering plants and a shady spot for a dog or two. And a fountain. I love the sound of water."

The kids got to the steep, but paved sidewalk that led down to the covered bridge. It was early evening and the sun was still out, but getting low in the sky. Since it was nearing dinner time, there weren't any people around. The park closed at dark, so they'd have to be quick.

A fisherman with all his gear was walking up the hill and

Finn asked, "Did you catch anything?"

"Not a one!" The fisherman replied.

"Good, it's not just me!" Finn joked as the man laughed and continued slowly up the steep slope.

The kids walked onto the covered bridge which was shaded and beautiful. Riley found the earthy smell of the wooden railroad ties forming the open walls to be comforting. She was always drawn to the beauty of the creek below them and they all stopped to watch the rushing water. Riley was mesmerized by the light bouncing off the water, making it almost sparkle.

"I think it's so cool they built this bridge to look like an old one," Riley said as they continued walking to the end of the bridge.

"It's so beautiful." Eve looked up at the vaulted roof line fashioned with honey-colored wood.

After the kids crossed the bridge, they went to the path on the left with Molly leading the way. It was a steep, rocky, rooted path, but since many people used it, it wasn't dangerous if you walked slowly. Molly climbed down it very easily with her four legs, looking up at Riley and Eve as if to say, "What's taking you so long?"

Molly loved these trails, her nose was going a mile-a-minute, as she sniffed the plants along the dirt path. The kids crossed under the bridge, heading down the straight path toward the bend in the creek.

"It's going to get dark soon, we better be quick." Riley was anxious to get out of there. She knew the park wasn't regularly patrolled, but rules are rules and she didn't really want to be here after dark anyway. After all, it was still warm enough for snakes.

Finn stopped and said, "Here, this is where we found the dog." He crouched next to a rock along the bank where there was still a clump of leaves and debris, and pointed to it.

Eve crouched next to Finn and was looking at the spot when Molly started to growl-a deep, low growl. Riley, who was still standing, looked around and turned in the direction Molly was looking - behind them and up the steep hill.

"What is it, girl?" Finn stood up and patted Molly on the back.

"Finn, look, up there!" Riley said in a nervous whisper. "At ten o'clock, there's a person."

Finn adjusted his gaze to the left and further up the hill. "I see him." He tried to settle Molly, "It's okay, girl," he said as quietly as he could and stroked Molly's back, she was still growling low, her hackles were raised. He turned to Eve, "Eve, we gotta get outta here. Do you sense anything?"

Before Eve could answer, Molly pulled so hard on the leash, it jerked right out of Finn's hand. "Molly, no!" Finn yelled, but it was too late, she was already halfway up the hill, her leash trailing behind her.

The hill was too steep for the kids to climb up, so they had to go back the way they came. Finn sprinted toward the covered bridge with Riley on his heels. Eve was slower than them and about six feet behind them. The hill was harder to climb up now that they were in a hurry and frantic. Finn steadied himself on tree limbs as he clambered up, Riley followed suit.

Finn and Riley reached the top of the hill and climbed the steep cement steps to where the nature trail began. "Molly!" Finn yelled as loud as he could, he was freaking out inside.

"Molly! Come here, girl!" Riley called out as loud as she could, "Moll-eee!"

They climbed up the steep, rocky, rooted slope where the trail forked off.

"Which way?" Riley asked Finn who was scanning the dim landscape. Just then, they heard Molly barking off to their left, down the trail that led to the dam.

"This way!" Finn said as Eve had just made it up the steep trail. "Come on, Eve!"

They were quickly losing light and couldn't see Molly, but Riley knew they must be going in the right direction because Molly's barks were getting louder. "Come on, let's go!" Riley sped up her pace.

"Be careful," Finn said, "there's lots of rocks and roots."

No sooner had he said that, then Riley caught her toe on one or the other and went flying, landing on her palms and knees. "Ouch!" Molly's barking had become more frantic, so Riley jumped up and sprinted to catch up to Finn ignoring the burning sensation from skinning her hands and knees on the dirt.

They were getting closer to Molly's frantic barking and then it happened, they heard a shot, and Molly's barking ceased. Finn and Riley stopped dead in their tracks.

Riley gasped and Finn grabbed her arm to steady himself. Eve caught up to them with a look of sheer panic on her face. "Did you hear that?" She whispered so only her friends could hear her. "Was that a gun?"

Finn was looking in every direction, trying to decide which way to go, silently praying that Molly would be okay. He was still holding onto Riley's arm, all three of them standing still as statues, their ears tuned in to every little noise. They could hear the tree frogs chiming like a symphony. They could hear the rushing of the water which meant they were close to the dam. They heard everything ...except Molly.

# CHAPTER THIRTEEN

## In Trouble Again

Finn felt like his heart was going to pound out of his chest and his eyes stung. He took a deep breath and told himself to focus. "We need to keep going. We have to find her, even if…" He couldn't bear to say it out loud.

"Come on, Molly," Riley whispered, as they continued down the trail. "Where are you girl?"

"Shh, do you hear that?" Finn asked.

"Yes," Eve whispered, "I hear whimpering."

"It's Molly, she's alive!" Riley said, as quietly as she could, though she could have screamed with joy.

"Let's go! This way!" Finn said as he headed down the trail closer to the dam.

The kids got to the dam and followed Molly's whimpering. Finn looked to his right, up the slope, where he just barely made out Molly's body lying on the ground near a felled tree. He immediately ran up the hill and over to her, she was still whimpering.

"Molly, are you okay?" He asked as he ran his hands along her body, frantically but gently searching for injuries.

Riley scrambled up the slope and knelt down next to Finn. "Is she okay?"

"I don't know, I can't tell."

"Here." Riley pulled her phone out of the back pocket of

her jeans. She tapped the screen a few times and the flashlight came on. Riley waved the flashlight over Molly's mostly black and tan fur, but they couldn't see anything. Her head looked fine, so did her back and sides. "I can't see anything." Riley's hand was trembling.

Finn found Molly's leash which was wrapped underneath her. He pulled the leash out from under her, all the while she was still whimpering and whining. "Come on, girl, let's go," Finn said as he tugged gently on her leash.

Molly wouldn't budge and was focused on something, but what? Finn pulled at the leash again. "Come on, Molly, let's go." But Molly wasn't going anywhere and she began pawing at the dirt and brush.

Riley stroked Molly's back, hoping to herself that she might see something.

"Do you see anything?" Finn whispered.

"No, sorry." Riley wished she had. She continued to stroke Molly's dark fur, trying to comfort both herself and the dog.

Eve was looking in the direction Molly was looking and she noticed something. There was a tangle of brush that looked like it had been disturbed. "I do."

"What? What do you see?" Riley asked, feeling as if her stomach was now on fire from nerves.

"It's a dog. The spirit of a dog. A white one." Eve's eyes were looking at something and nothing at the same time. "I think it's under this brush." She nodded to the area just in front of Molly's dirt-caked paws.

Both girls were too nervous to move, so Finn started to gently move the leaves and sticks until he uncovered a dog.

Another white dog, like the one from the creek. He pulled some leaves out of the soft, fine fur and felt knots and tangles. There were knots all over this dog, and feces in its fur. Riley felt like she was going to throw up. "This dog is in bad shape." Finn slowly rolled the dog over and found blood and a bullet hole in the dog's side, near her heart.

Riley turned to Eve, "We have to call your dad."

"No, we can't…," Eve stood up, "I'll get in so much trouble."

"Eve, we don't have a choice." Finn wiped his hands on his pants and stood up.

"Yeah, it's bad enough we found the dog in the creek, now we find another white dog that looks the same and it's been shot. Probably by that person we saw up the hill." Riley's voice grew quiet as she said this, she looked around, scanning the dense woods, hoping he wasn't watching them from somewhere.

"She's right," Finn whispered, "he could still be here."

"What should we do about the dog?" Riley asked. "Leave it here or take it with us?"

"It's a crime scene," Eve replied, "we should leave it where it is."

"But what if whoever shot it takes it before we can get your dad back here? He could be watching us." Riley was trying to be as quiet as possible her nerves were making her stomach upset and her imagination was going wild.

"Give me your phone," Finn said to Riley who handed it over. He took a few pictures of the dog to show Mr. Rycroft in case the dog disappeared before they got back. "I think Eve is right, we have to leave it where it is, and we're not safe here. Remember what that voice said on the recording?"

"Be careful. Oh my gosh…" Eve said, realizing they probably were being warned.

"How are we going to find this spot to show Eve's dad?" Riley asked. "We're lost and it's too dark."

"Hang on, I think I've got something." Finn reached into one of the pockets of his cargo pants. He always seemed to be prepared with something that he could fashion into what they needed. "Here it is," he said as he found something deep in the pocket. He held up a piece of white chalk. "We'll mark the trees and rocks with it as we leave, that way we can find our way back."

"Great idea," Riley said.

"Yeah," Eve said, "now let's get out of here, I'm getting creeped out."

Since it clearly wasn't safe to stay in the park, the kids went to the closest place where there would be people, Mill Street Grounds, the coffee shop at the top of Mill Street. They were so scared, they ran all the way. Mr. Rycroft was already waiting for them and was not happy.

"Why are you out at dark on a school night?"

"Um…well," Riley started and looked at Eve.

Eve was too scared to say anything so Finn piped up, "We have to show you something. Can you drive down to the covered bridge?"

"What is going on? You three shouldn't be anywhere near the park this late by yourselves."

Riley was so scared because she knew Mr. Rycroft was really angry. "We found another dog."

"Is it alive?" Mr. Rycroft asked with hesitation in his voice.

"It was," Eve said.

### 

Mr. Rycroft drove the kids and Molly to a parking space right near the entrance to the path that led to the bridge. Since it was now dark, there were very few cars in the lot. He turned on his interior light, looked at his daughter and said, "Eve, what's going on? Why would you come down here when you know you're not allowed?"

Finn and Riley exchanged nervous glances in the backseat as Molly sat in between them panting.

"Um, well, I kinda asked Finn and Riley to show me the spot where they found the other dog. I wondered if I could see its spirit…," Eve said.

"You know you aren't supposed to go on these trails without me. These woods are thick, you don't know who's out here, Eve. It's dangerous."

"I know dad, I'm sorry. I just thought I might be able to help." Eve fidgeted with her fingernails, unable to look her dad in the eyes.

Finn and Riley filled Mr. Rycroft in on the whole story and this seemed to upset him even more. "See, I told you how dangerous it can be out here! You heard gun fire, out here in the woods, near dark!" He looked at Finn and Riley and said, "Do your parents know what's going on?"

"Not yet sir," Riley said. "We were so scared and we knew we had to call you." She pulled out her phone. "Shoot, my ringer was off." Riley was looking through her phone's call log. "I missed calls from my house and Finn's."

"You need to call them now so they know where you are and ask their permission for you to show me where you found the dog." Mr. Rycroft was trying to stay calm, but was so upset that the kids had been careless and could have been hurt.

Finn's and Riley's parents were really angry with them but gave them permission to show Mr. Rycroft the crime scene and then asked that he bring them home immediately after. It looked like everyone was in trouble tonight.

### 

When the kids, Molly, and Mr. Rycroft got down to the covered bridge, Molly started to growl, low and steady. Finn clenched her leash tightly this time and wrapped it around his hand a couple of times.

"I see shadows at the end of the bridge," Riley whispered just as they heard something splash into the rushing creek.

Mr. Rycroft clicked on his flashlight which seemed to light up the whole bridge. At the end of the bridge were three figures, Corey Thornton along with Brad and Seth. "Kids, what are you doing down here? The park closes at dark."

Corey slid his backpack back onto his shoulders and said, "We were just heading home."

"What did you just throw into the creek?" Riley said to Corey, finding boldness from her anger.

"A rock," Corey said with a smirk.

"That's dangerous," Mr. Rycroft said. "Don't throw things off of this bridge. Ever. Now, you boys get along. Park's closed."

The three boys muttered something under their breath, but Riley couldn't make it out. As the boys passed them, Corey said so only Riley could hear, "It's not like I was throwing a dead body off the bridge."

Riley shuddered. He was bad news. Really bad news.

After Corey and his friends were out of sight, they headed to where the kids had found Molly and the dog. Thankfully between Mr. Rycroft's powerful flashlight and Finn's chalk marks, they were able to find the spot fairly quickly. They all climbed the steep slope up to where the dog was laying.

Finn pointed to the pile of brush, "That's where we found it." Mr. Rycroft slowly moved the debris away, but nothing was there. He shined his flashlight around the ground and saw a small area of blood. He took out a plastic bag and scooped up some of the dirt where the blood was. He then shined his light all around the area, looking for any other evidence, but found nothing. The area was so dense with plant life that it was hard to find any footprints at all.

Mr. Rycroft let out a loud sign, "The body's gone and I need to get you three home. There's not much more I can do right now."

"Wait, the pictures! Finn took pictures because he and Eve said it was a crime scene and we shouldn't move the dog. I knew that man was still here," Riley said as she showed the photos to Mr. Rycroft.

"Yeah, I even took one from further away so you could see the area," Finn said as he stood on the other side of Eve's dad to show him. "It's the last one, see, here it is," he said as Riley scrolled to the last photo. "Here's this stump here, and see that log in the distance? This is the spot and that's the dog."

Mr. Rycroft touched the screen to zoom in. Sure enough, there was a dog, a white one just like the one from last week. "Well, whoever did this took the body. Riley, will you email these pictures to me?"

"Sure, Mr. Rycroft. Do you think he's still here?" She looked around and got a chill up her spine.

"I'm sure whoever did this is long gone. Don't worry, I'm going to call this in and get you three home. I'll come back out and see what we can find."

Mr. Rycroft led the kids down to the trail. Once on the trail, Riley grabbed Finn's arm to slow him down. She whispered to him, "Is it just me, or is Mr. Rycroft acting kinda weird?"

Finn thought for a moment. "I think it's just his anger at what we did, and what could have happened to us." Riley hoped that Finn was right.

# CHAPTER FOURTEEN

## *Like Father, Like Son*

After their adventure in the woods, Riley, Finn, and Eve were all grounded…for one month. All their parents were mad, even Mr. and Mrs. Murphy who were normally very lenient. Finn thought it had more to do with the gunshot than the fact that they were at the creek close to dark. Whatever was going on in their little town, it was getting serious and all three families knew it.

Riley was glad that she and Finn at least had time on school days to hang out and discuss what was going on in Roswell. As they walked to school the next day, they discussed the events at the park when Riley stopped in her tracks in front of the church. "What's up?" Finn asked.

"That dog we found."

"Yeah, what about…" Finn stopped himself, realizing what had just dawned on Riley. "The dog we found!"

"Yep! Looks just like the two other dogs we've found, doesn't it?" Riley was smiling now.

"It does! We have to find it!"

"But how?"

"Why didn't I think of this sooner?" Finn asked himself out loud.

"You can ask your mom to check with Rhonda. Maybe she'll know who adopted the dog?"

"That's a great idea!" Finn said as he pulled out his phone to call his mom. There was a pause after he dialed his mom's number.

Riley listened as Finn spoke with his mom, eager to find out what she was saying. As soon as he clicked his phone off she said, "What'd she say?"

"She said she'd check with Rhonda, but she wasn't sure they were allowed to give out information on who adopted from them."

Riley's heart sank. "Yeah, I can kinda see that. Too bad."

"I know, but we can still look!" Finn said.

"Have you already forgotten we've been grounded for a month? It'll practically be Thanksgiving before we can even do anything."

"Well, after our grounding is over, let's search dog parks and see what we can find. You never know!" Finn said. Riley loved how optimistic he was.

### 

A few weeks into her punishment, Riley was sitting on the front porch drawing since she had finished her chores and homework and had nothing else to do. Normally she'd be riding bikes with Finn, or in the park with Finn and Molly. Her dad came out onto the porch with his car keys in hand.

"Hey Roo," he said, "what are you up to?"

"Not much, dad. Just hanging out and drawing. Enjoying the nice weather." Riley was slowly rocking back and forth, behind the row of boxwoods that lined the front of the porch.

"I've got to run up to Roswell Hardware, do you want to come with me?"

Riley was happy to get to spend any kind of time with her dad, so she jumped at the chance. "Sure!" She hopped out of the rocking chair which continued to rock back and forth.

"Great, after we're done there, we'll go to the Public House for a little something to eat." Riley's dad was happy to get one on one time with his youngest daughter. "Come on, we'll drive today."

### 

The old hardware store had been located in historic Roswell since just after the Civil War and Riley's dad preferred it to the big box stores. The inventory might have been slightly more expensive, but he was old fashioned and liked the service you got at Roswell Hardware–kind and thoughtful. As they walked into the store, the old brass bell announced their arrival and Paul Durham, the great-great-great grandson of the original owner, George Durham, greeted them with a warm "hello."

"Hi there, Paul. How's business?" Riley's dad asked.

"Oh, it's pretty good, thanks. Are you looking for anything in particular?"

"I just need to pick up some stainless steel lag bolts."

"Sure thing. They are on the last row in the far corner. Do you want me to take you?"

"Nah, Riley and I will find them, and do a little browsing, thanks."

Riley and her dad walked across the old wooden floors

which creaked in certain spots. Riley loved coming here because it was old and she thought of all the stories this place could tell.

"That's why I like this place, Roo," Riley's dad said as they found the buckets of all kinds of hardware. "Family-owned and operated since the 1800's and you get quality service. You can't find that in many places these days."

"I like it because it's old," Riley said as she dug through a bin of washers, "and it smells good in here."

Riley's dad laughed as he tousled his daughter's hair. "You are one of a kind, my dear, and that's one reason why I love you so much."

Riley smiled up at her dad. She wished they had more time to spend together.

Just then, her dad stiffened as he seemed to notice someone. "Hadrian, how are you?" Riley's dad called out to his colleague and son of one of Roswell's first families. Hadrian Thornton had appeared at the other end of the aisle.

Riley noticed that her dad's smile seemed forced, and that Mr. Thornton's seemed plastic. He was wearing a long khaki trench coat over a pair of dark brown corduroys, and a blue Oxford button down.

"Doing just fine, Jack," Mr. Thornton said, still looking like plastic-man.

"I think you know my daughter, Riley. She and Corey are in the same grade."

"Oh, yes, hello," Mr. Thornton said, but Riley didn't think he cared or even wanted to be bothered with her and her dad. At that moment, a man with a slight limp walked around the corner behind Mr. Thornton.

"Hey Jed," Riley's dad said to the man who joined Mr. Thornton.

Riley thought Jed looked about the same age as her dad and Mr. Thornton, but looked like life hadn't been as easy on him. He said "hello" then said something to Mr. Thornton, his eyes partially shielded by the brim of his grimy orange and blue cap. He showed Mr. Thornton the wire clamps he was holding in his hand. Riley thought he was probably too scared to say anything more to them in front of Mr. Thornton in case it sounded bad or embarrassed him. She figured everyone in the family was as miserable as Corey so she could understand his lack of common courtesy.

"Well, we've got what we need to make some repairs. See you at the office tomorrow," Mr. Thornton said as he and Jed turned the corner and headed to the cash register.

"That was weird," Riley said to her dad. "That man with Mr. Thornton seemed scared of him."

"That's Jed Clinton, he and Hadrian were friends in high school and now Jed is the Thornton's estate manger."

"Why does he need one of those?" Riley asked as she plucked some nuts and bolts out of a bin while her dad searched for the right lag bolts.

"The Thorntons have a lot of property, and when Jed hurt himself and couldn't play football anymore, Hadrian's dad made sure to give Jed work to do and Mr. Thornton has continued to help him."

"Wow, someone in the Thornton family cares that much for another person who isn't even a family member? I wonder how that happened?" Riley said, thinking of Corey and what a nasty boy he was.

"The summer before their senior year in high school, Hadrian and Jed were in a bad car accident. Jed supposedly saved Hadrian's life that night. It was also the night that ended Jed's football career. He broke his leg so bad he couldn't play anymore. He was heavily recruited and many thought he would have been good enough to go pro."

"You said, 'supposedly', was there any doubt that Jed saved Mr. Thornton?" Riley asked.

"Well, there were stories, but you know I've never been into gossip."

"Well Mr. Thornton seems kinda fake and since I've had plenty of experience with Corey, I'm not a big fan of that family."

Riley's dad laughed at what his daughter had said. "We get along because we have to. Truth be told, I've saved his butt a few times on cases where his work was sloppy, but he gets away with a lot because of the family name."

"That's not fair." Riley stopped playing with nuts and bolts and turned to her dad who seemed surprisingly okay with what he had just told her.

"Well, Roo," her dad plucked the hardware he needed out of a bin, "life's not fair. You just have to do right by yourself, do the right thing, and hope it all works out in the end." He smiled at his sweet daughter and hoped the unfairness of life wouldn't break her heart some day.

"Okay, but it's still not fair," Riley said as she tossed the nuts and bolts back into their bins.

"I know, honey." Her dad put his arm around Riley's

shoulder and they headed to the cash register.

After Mr. Carson paid for his purchase, he and Riley headed next door to the Public House restaurant. The Public House was located in a building that dated back to 1854 and faced the town square. The lunch rush had come and gone and there were just a few tables occupied. The friendly, young hostess took Riley and her dad to a seat in front of one of the huge windows that looked out at the square and busy Atlanta Street.

As they looked at their menus, Riley said, "You know this place is supposed to be haunted?"

"Michael and Catherine," Riley's dad said, referring to the young Union soldier and his forbidden love with the Southern Roswell resident whose family obviously supported the Confederacy.

"How did you know?"

"I'm not just a boring lawyer." Riley's dad laughed, "Remember, I grew up here too, and this was once my stomping ground."

"So do you think it's true?"

"Well, the story has been around for so long and so many people talk of experiencing things in this building, I think it probably is true."

"Falling in love with someone on the opposite side of the Civil War must have been tough," Riley said.

"I'm sure it was. If Michael and Catherine couldn't be together in life, perhaps they do haunt this place so they can always be together in a place that is special for them."

After a few minutes, the waitress came by and took their order. Riley was looking out the window, watching the traffic fly by.

"Penny for your thoughts?" Her dad said.

"I was just thinking of what it must have been like back when Michael and Catherine were alive. It's so busy now. I bet Roswell was so different."

"It certainly was. The town was still very young, of course, so was Atlanta," Riley's dad said as the waitress brought their drinks and headed back toward the kitchen, her pony tail swinging from side to side as she walked.

"It's sad to think of how much Sherman burned around here. I guess we should consider it really lucky he didn't burn all of Roswell, like he did Atlanta," Riley said.

"We're very fortunate to have some history left here in Roswell," Riley's dad said as something caught his eye across the street.

Riley followed her dad's gaze to the square. It was a bit elevated from where they were sitting, and she could see two men having a heated discussion near the fountain. "Is that Mr. Thornton and his estate manager?"

"Looks like it."

"I wonder what they are arguing about?" Riley thought aloud.

"It's Hadrian. Jed probably trimmed a shrub too short and is getting a tongue-lashing." Riley's dad gave her a wink.

"So he is as miserable as Corey." Riley figured there couldn't be a nice person anywhere in that family.

"He's a pretty tough guy. Not the easiest guy to work for or with."

"You'd think he'd be a little easier on the guy who supposedly saved his life," Riley said as the waitress appeared with their food.

Riley's dad looked at his young daughter and said, "Enough talk about the Thorntons, let's dig in and talk about something more appetizing."

"Let's talk some more about the ghosts. What other stories do you know?"

"Roo, you really are starting to sound like Finn! Hasn't he told you all the stories by now?"

"Probably, but you've been around here way longer, you may know some that Finn doesn't, and boy would I love to tell him a story he hasn't heard before!"

"Way longer? Thanks a lot!"

Riley was grinning as she cut a piece of her crepe that was oozing hot melted chocolate. "You know what I mean, dad!"

Riley's dad was happy. It was little moments like this that made his heart feel like it was literally growing. It also made him wonder if breaking his back working for a huge law firm was worth it. He quickly put that thought out of his head and tried to think of ghost stories that would stump even the master ghost aficionado, Finn Murphy. He was going to enjoy this moment, work would come soon enough. He stole a glance back out the window. Hadrian clearly wasn't happy.

# CHAPTER FIFTEEN

# The Mystery Man

After Riley and Finn were cleared from being grounded, they were on a mission to find the dog from the first day of school. They took Molly to dog parks and regular parks, at least any they could walk to, and searched for the little white dog. For weeks the two kids searched for that dog, but didn't find her. "You know, that dog could be anywhere…even a different town," Riley said.

"Yeah, and since the rescue group can't give out information on who has it, it's like finding a needle in a haystack."

"If we can't find it, then we can't help Mr. Rycroft with this case. I mean, I think if I touch the dog, maybe I can find out if it's connected to the other two," Riley said. "Maybe I can find out *something*."

"I know. I just keep thinking about that EVP we captured. Maybe we just need to be careful and let the police handle this," Finn said.

"It's just nagging at me. I want to find that dog."

"We can't say we didn't try. You know how sometimes if you step back from a problem, you can figure it out easier? Maybe that's what we need to do."

"Well, since Thanksgiving break is coming up and you'll be in Florida, maybe it'll be a good time to do that." Riley was a little disappointed that Finn didn't share her passion for finding the dog. Maybe I'm obsessing too much about it, she thought.

### 

On the last day of school before Thanksgiving break, Finn and Riley walked home together as usual. Finn still seemed worried about Riley's need to find the dog from the first day of school, even though they had given up actively looking for it. "I kinda wish we weren't going to Florida so you don't go looking for the dog on your own," Finn said, referring to his family's yearly trip to see his grandparents in Clearwater, Florida for Thanksgiving.

"Oh, come on, you love going to see your grandparents! Don't worry, I'll wait to have any adventure until you get back." Riley smiled at her best friend who loved adventure and problem solving more than anyone she knew.

"You better!" He said with a grin, then stopped and looked at her, "Promise me you'll be safe."

"I'll be safe." Riley felt her face grow hot and looked at her sneakers. "Don't worry, I don't want to be grounded again." She smiled and tucked her hair behind her ear.

Even though Riley told Finn she wouldn't have any adventure without him, she couldn't stop thinking about the dog from the first day of school. She was obsessing, she knew it, but she felt in her gut that it had to be connected.

### 

The day before Thanksgiving was unseasonably warm

which wasn't uncommon in Roswell, and Riley was bored. She decided to take a bike ride to clear her head and enjoy the beautiful weather. As she approached the square, she decided to cross Atlanta Street and head down to the covered bridge. She knew she shouldn't go there on her own, but something was pulling her there. The area was busy since school was out and most people were off work; there were lots of families enjoying the trails around the creek. Riley locked her bike up at the entrance to the park and headed down the steep path toward the bridge. There were lots of dogs at this park today, but so far, none that looked like the ones she and Finn had found, most were large dogs hiking with their owners. Riley crossed the bridge, stopping to admire the beauty of the rushing water and savoring the sound of the flowing creek. It was a sight that never got old.

As she was standing on the bridge, enjoying the view, Riley got a cold chill. She shuddered and looked toward the spot where she and Finn had found the dog along the bank of the creek. That section of the path was empty, it seemed most people were on the other side of the creek or up on the trails high above the creek. Riley decided to head down to the spot where she and Finn found the dog. She crossed the bridge and walked down to the trail which ran along the south side of the creek. She crossed back under the bridge and walked next to the large sewer pipe that ran along this section of the path. One aspect of the trails she didn't like were the pipes that ran along and across the creek. She made a mental note to ask her dad what they were for, hoping it wasn't for sewer waste.

As Riley got to the bend in the creek, she paused where they had found the poor dead dog. She said a silent prayer that the dog was now at peace and that she would be able to figure out what had happened to the dogs that looked so much alike. I've got to figure out what's going on here, she thought, her throat tightened and she blinked back tears just thinking about the poor dog they found here.

Riley continued walking to where the creek hooked and headed south toward the Chattahoochee River. At the hook in the creek, she turned and realized there wasn't really a path that continued down the creek at this point. To her right was the creek and to her left was a steep slope upward where she knew the trail system wound high above her. Riley stopped and looked around while the creek flowed quickly next to her. She spotted something white about ten yards down the bank and carefully started walking toward it. The mud was thick here and the terrain rocky and slippery. As she neared the white object, her heart pounded and as she craned her neck to see what it was, she slipped on a rock but quickly regained her balance. To her relief, it was a plastic grocery bag. Thank goodness, she thought. Normally she would have picked it up to throw it away, but she was still a good distance from it and it was too dangerous to go any further. She carefully turned to head back toward the real path, took one step, caught her toe on a rock, and slipped. This time, Riley couldn't regain her balance, she fell to her left and plunged into the fast moving creek, hitting her tail bone on a submerged rock.

It was cold, icier than she thought it would be and the current was swift. Riley was a good swimmer, but she was disoriented and in pain from hitting that rock. She was grasping for a rock or a limb, anything to stop from staying in this creek.

She was getting so tossed around by the current that she kept breathing in water. Normally water never scared Riley, but she was panicking. The current kept tossing her under the water and she was sucking it in, choking and coughing, all the while, her body was scraping against rocks in the creek. Riley was desperately trying to grab something to stop herself and she was now facing backwards. She was trying to right herself so she could see where she was going when something grabbed her wrist. Riley was yanked out of the water and on to the muddy creek bank. She was on her back coughing up water and felt a shadow come in front of the sun and looked up. There was a tall, broad shouldered man with deep, dark skin standing over her with a look of worry in his large, brown eyes, his brow was furrowed.

Riley was coughing and gasping for air from the water she inhaled. When she was finally able to breathe, she said, "Thank you. Thank you so much." She coughed some more and was able to sit up, her teeth chattering.

The man pulled a handkerchief out of the pocket of his tattered cotton pants and wiped the water off Riley's forehead. He put his hand on her shoulder and she immediately felt warmth. "Child, you need ta be more careful. You coulda got hurt."

"I know, I'm sorry," Riley said, feeling disoriented and wheezing from the water still stuck in her windpipe. "The dogs. I've got to find out…what's happening to them." She closed her eyes, willing herself not to cry.

"You will, child, you will. But you listen ta me. You got ta be careful. *Real* careful," the man said as he put his handkerchief back in his pocket.

Riley rubbed her eyes and looked up at the man who had

just saved her life, but he was gone. She sprang to her feet and looked around. There wasn't a soul to be found.

"Hello? Sir? Do you know about the dogs?" Riley called out, but no response came. She wiped her hair out of her eyes and turned in a circle. She said to herself, where did he go? While her clothes were indeed wet, she wasn't cold anymore. She looked at her feet and saw her footprints in the mud, along with much larger ones. "What just happened?" She asked herself aloud. While she was frightened about her fall into the creek and nearly drowning, she was also comforted by the man who saved her. The man who seemed to have disappeared into thin air.

# CHAPTER SIXTEEN

## *Encounter with Evan*

Riley ran out of the park as quickly as she could and tried not to draw anyone's attention. Like that was even possible. She knew she must look like a mess and really didn't want to have to explain herself to anyone who was trying to be helpful. She just wanted to get home. The quickest route was to go up Mill Street, but it had a really steep hill, one that Riley had trouble riding her bike up on a good day. She got as far as she could and then hopped off her bike and started walking it up, her wet sneakers made a squishing sound as she walked. She was glad the sun was out as it helped to warm her, but she was starting to feel cold to the bone again, her jeans and long sleeved t-shirt soaking wet. Her experience in the creek and the man who saved her was running through her head. She was trying to make sense of it, wondering if she was just delusional and made up this seemingly invisible man. Maybe it was lack of oxygen to the brain? She heard squeaking brakes pull up next to her and a loud engine which brought her back to reality.

"Riley? You okay?"

Riley looked at the driver of the old Ford Bronco with peeling blue paint and saw that it was Eve's brother, Evan. "Oh, hey. Yeah, just heading home," she said as she tucked her hair behind her ear, and tried to play it cool.

"Ah…what happened to you? Did you fall in the creek or

something?" Evan asked, putting his car in park and pulling up on the emergency brake.

"Um, yeah...actually, I did," Riley blushed. "Please don't tell your dad, my parents will kill me if they found out I was hanging out there alone."

Evan got out of his truck and opened the passenger door. "Here, get in and crank up the heat, I'll put your bike on the rack," he said as he pointed to the bike rack on the back of his Bronco.

Riley noticed that aside from looking gorgeous, he looked really concerned, his brow was furrowed and he was moving quickly which made her think she must have looked much worse than she realized. Riley hopped into the truck and turned the heat on high. It felt like heaven.

Evan got in and reached into the back seat. He grabbed a worn brown leather jacket and handed it to Riley. "Here, put this on. It's all I've got, but it should help you warm up." As he drove the truck up the hill toward the intersection where the light was red, he said, "So, are you sure you're okay?"

"Yeah, really, I'm fine." Riley pulled her arms through the jacket and hugged it around her torso, her teeth were chattering. "I was hanging out at the creek and...thought I saw something further up the bank, went to check it out, and I slipped and fell. I got caught up in the water, but I, uh...managed to get out."

"Man, that's scary." The light finally changed to green and Evan went straight through the intersection then turned right on Mimosa.

"Yeah, it was, but I'm okay." Riley thought it was nice that Evan was so concerned and she didn't remember him being this cute when he was over at their house. She was glad she wasn't far from home, though, because she really needed to get warm and dry.

"I won't say anything to anyone, but you can't go hanging out at the creek by yourself. You're really lucky you got out of there on your own, without anyone around to help you, and without getting hurt. I swear between the last incident and today, someone must be watching over you."

Riley sensed a tone of sadness in his words. "I know. It was stupid for me to go by myself, and yes, I'm really lucky. I must have a guardian angel." She didn't like being even the slightest bit dishonest and felt bad for not telling the whole truth, but she couldn't even explain what had happened.

"What did you think you saw on the bank, anyway?"

Riley wondered why he sounded so interested and really just wanted to get home. "Um, I thought, maybe it was an animal or something, but it was just a plastic bag, thank goodness."

"Oh, good. Alright, here we are," he said as he pulled in front of her house. "If your parents see my car and ask me what happened, I'm going to be honest with them."

"I understand." Riley didn't want to get anyone else in trouble and wished the Bronco's engine and brakes weren't so loud.

"Go get a hot shower and eat some soup or something. You need to warm up," Evan said.

"Okay, I will." She felt stupid and like a dumb kid compared to Evan. She hung her head, embarrassed he found her, but glad he did. She was freezing.

Riley was getting out of the car and Evan was rummaging through some junk in his car. He pulled out a pen and tore a corner off an envelope. Here, this is my cell number. Text me to let me know you're okay."

Riley felt for her phone in her back pockets, a look of panic crossed her face.

Evan noticed her reaction, "Did you lose your phone in the creek?" He got out of the car to help her with her bike.

She thought about it for a moment. "I don't know, I…No, I think I left it on my dresser! Oh, I hope I left it there, otherwise my parents will kill me." She grabbed her bike from Evan.

"I don't think they'll kill you, but you will have to fess up. However you do it, just text me to let me know you're okay, alright?" Riley knew she must look horrible by the way Evan was looking at her and insisting she let him know she was alright.

"I will…" Riley was looking at her wet, muddy sneakers, "…and thanks again. I really appreciate you taking me home."

"No problem," Evan said with a grin, "now get inside and warm up before you get hypothermia."

"Will do." Riley turned and wheeled her bike into the garage and waved goodbye. She really hoped no one was around so she could just try to forget this day ever happened.

By the grace of God, Riley's mom and Hailey were watching a movie in the basement media room and her dad was working at the office. Riley snuck upstairs and showered without anyone being the wiser. When she got out of the shower, she saw her phone on the dresser and fished inside the pocket of Evan's jacket for his number. She texted him, *All's well, no hypothermia, thanks again!*

Riley set her phone on her nightstand and picked Evan's jacket back up. It smelled good, like leather and sandalwood.

Then she thought about Eve and it dawned on her. Why is Evan here? Shouldn't he be in Savannah with Eve and their dad? This didn't make any sense to Riley, but she settled onto her bed, under her favorite blanket and quickly fell asleep, only waking when she smelled dinner cooking downstairs. Her ordeal at the creek had clearly worn her out more than she realized and was starving when she went downstairs to join her family. She thought of Evan again and why he was here, not in Savannah with his family.

# CHAPTER SEVENTEEN

## Lucy Mae Powell

On Thanksgiving morning, Riley rode her bike to the Rycrofts to give Evan his jacket back but he wasn't there. She was kind of glad because she had felt awkward enough yesterday. She left his jacket on the porch and sent him a text that it was there. She was glad to put yesterday behind her and enjoyed Thanksgiving with her family. It was a nice distraction from all the recent drama.

### ###

On the Saturday after Thanksgiving, Riley went to lunch with her mom and Hailey in historic downtown Roswell. Since it was a nice autumn day, the three walked from their house off Mimosa to Canton street where you couldn't throw a stone without hitting a good restaurant. The area was always busy on nice weekend days and nights, and today was no exception. All three Carson women loved Table & Main, so Priscilla decided she would treat them to lunch at their favorite spot. The menu was fresh food with a southern flair and usually the girls shared the fried chicken. It was always a struggle to decide on which side to get, but it usually ended up being mac and cheese. The three were seated at a table by a window at the front of the restaurant and Riley loved people-watching as her mom and sister talked about fashion and make-up. They had just finished their fried okra appetizer when Riley hopped up from the table. "Oh, my gosh!"

"Riley, what is it?" Her mom asked quietly as she looked around to make sure the whole restaurant wasn't looking at her impulsive daughter.

Riley tossed her napkin on her chair, "I think it's the dog we found! Be right back!" And she was off.

Priscilla and Hailey watched as Riley went out the door, dashed across the porch, and down the brick walk way to the sidewalk. There was an older lady with white hair who had a little white dog on a pink leash.

"I swear, she is so embarrassing," Hailey said as she grabbed a cheese straw from a small mason jar on the table. "What is she doing, anyway?"

Riley's mom, whose back was to the window, turned in her chair for a second to see what her youngest daughter was doing. "I don't know," she said as she turned back around, "maybe it's that dog she's been going on about. She and Finn found a stray on the first day of school and she said they needed to find it. I honestly don't know why. You know your sister, she's crazy about dogs."

"Crazy in general, but what's so special about this one?" Hailey asked as she was looking at her phone.

"I don't know. Honey, please, put that phone away. You know I can't stand it when you kids get on your phones at the table. I know it's the 21st century, but we can still have manners."

"Yeah, like Riley who just jumped up and ran to talk to some old lady with a dog," Hailey said as she tucked her phone away.

"She's a model of decorum." She looked back out the window, "Is that Mrs. Powell she's talking to?"

Priscilla spun around in her seat, her eyes wide. "Lucy Mae Powell?"

"Yeah, I think that's her. We were just talking about the Powell family in history class. She's the last of the Powells living in Roswell, right?"

"Yes," Priscilla was unable to contain her excitement, "and she has been reclusive for the last few years!"

Lucy Mae Powell was related to one of the founding families of Roswell and because Priscilla Carson was keen to climb the social ladder in their town, she had been dying to meet Mrs. Powell for quite some time now.

"I have to go get your sister, there's no telling what she's doing. I don't want her giving us a bad name," Priscilla said as she hurriedly applied a fresh coat of lip gloss and headed out to her daughter.

### 

"Excuse me, ma'am," Riley said to the lady whose white dog was sniffing a dormant bush.

The older woman turned around and with a genial expression said, "Yes, dear?"

"Um, your dog, is he friendly?" Riley purposely called it a boy to find out if it could possibly be the female dog she and Finn had found.

"Thank you for asking. It's a she, Lily, and she is good with children and women. Would you like to pet her?"

"Yes, thank you, I just love dogs." Riley squatted down and held her hand out for the dog to sniff.

The little white dog trotted right over to Riley and she scratched the dog's chest. When she touched the dog, she felt hunger and darkness…and fear.

"Honey!" Riley's mom quickly headed toward Riley who hopped up quickly upon hearing her mother's voice. "I'm sure Mrs. Powell was on her way somewhere important, please don't keep her." Mrs. Carson extended her hand to Mrs. Powell and said, "Priscilla Carson, a pleasure to meet you. This is my youngest daughter, Riley. I'm sorry for the imposition, she just loves dogs, this one."

"Lucy Mae Powell, pleased to meet you, Priscilla, Riley." Mrs. Powell nodded to Riley, "It's okay, I love dogs, too."

Just then, Riley spotted Corey Thornton and his dad heading up the sidewalk and sweet little Lily turned into an angry little ball of fur, barking incessantly and pulling on her pink leash.

"Good afternoon, ladies," Mr. Thornton said tipping his fedora. "Mrs. Powell, Priscilla, so good to see you." He smiled and gave a cautious glance at Lily who was now hiding behind Mrs. Powell's legs, whimpering. "New dog?"

"Yes, I've rescued her and she's a bit traumatized," Mrs. Powell said, a little coolly, Riley thought.

Corey didn't say anything, but smirked at Riley and the little dog.

"Well, we won't stick around then." Mr. Thornton put his hand on Corey's back, leading him to keep heading down the sidewalk. "You ladies have a good day."

Riley's mom was saying something to Mr. Thornton about getting together with his wife and Mrs. Powell quietly said to Riley with a wink, "Dogs are always a good judge of character."

Riley smiled and replied so only Mrs. Powell could hear, "Lily must know that Corey and I are not friends."

After she finished talking to Mr. Thornton, Riley's mom said, "Mrs. Powell, it was so nice meeting you. We'd best let you finish your walk, and I think we've got some fried chicken waiting for us inside."

"Ooh, yum," Lucy Mae said, "my favorite! It was nice meeting you two as well." She looked at Riley and said, "It was so nice meeting you, dear. I do hope you come visit me sometime. Any young lady who loves dogs is a friend of mine."

"Thanks, Mrs. Powell, I'll do that!" Riley was excited and smiled from ear to ear.

Priscilla had to keep her mouth from hanging open. She couldn't believe it. She'd been trying to meet Mrs. Powell for years and her dog-loving daughter had just been invited to the lady's house, any time, because they both loved dogs! If she had known it was that easy...

# CHAPTER EIGHTEEN

## *An Invitation*

When Finn and Eve got back from Thanksgiving break, the three friends met at Mill Street Grounds and Riley told them all about her encounter with Mrs. Powell over hot chocolate. She told them what she felt when she touched the dog. She told them about how scared the dog was of Corey and Mr. Thornton and how Mrs. Powell invited her to come over, any time.

"Wow!" Finn said, "I can't believe you found the dog and that Mrs. Powell invited you over any time!"

"I know, how cool is that? I was about to give up and then when we were at lunch, I couldn't believe it! My mom said Mrs. Powell has been reclusive for the past few years. Ever since her husband died, she stopped going to events and parties. It's kinda sad."

"Then it's really special that she reached out to you," Eve said. "If she has been keeping to herself all these years, she must need a friend."

"Yeah, you need to go visit her!" Finn seemed to be back on the 'let's-find-out-what-happened-to-the-dogs' bandwagon again.

"I can't just show up at her house!" Riley tucked her hair behind her ear. "I think I'll write her a note. I think she would appreciate that."

"Good idea!" Finn said, "So, you said Lily was afraid of Mr.

Thornton and Corey. What did she do?"

"She was fine with me and my mom, but when they started heading towards us, she barked like crazy and was pulling at her leash. Then she cowered behind Mrs. Powell. Since Lily was going berserk, Corey and his dad didn't stick around."

"That's weird. I wonder what upset her?" Finn asked.

"Well, when I asked if Lily was friendly, Mrs. Powell said that she was fine with women and children. She must not like men for some reason."

"For some reason," Finn said. "If this dog is related to the other dogs we found, it has to be a man who's hurting them."

"Yeah," Eve said, "you need to meet with Mrs. Powell and see what you can find out. Maybe she has some insight."

"And if she doesn't," Finn said, "you could see if you can feel or see anything else when you touch Lily. It's too bad your mom came out right when you were feeling what Lily felt. We've got to figure out what's going on around here and I think that dog is our best chance."

"You're right. I'll write Mrs. Powell a note and have her call me if she'd like me to come over. I'll write it tonight and get it in the mail tomorrow."

### 

Three days had passed since Riley wrote to Mrs. Powell and she was sitting at the kitchen island, working on her homework as her mom fixed dinner; spaghetti and meatballs, Riley's favorite. As Riley was wrestling with a tough math problem, the phone rang and her mom grabbed it while she continued to stir the pasta.

"Hello?" Riley's mom sang into the phone, immediately getting flushed and excited. "Why hello, Mrs. Powell, how are you?"

Riley thought her mom looked like she might explode from excitement. Her lip-glossed smile was wide across her face and her eyes looked like they might just pop out of her blond head. Riley's mom naturally had a southern accent, but Riley swore it got thicker the moment her mom realized who was calling.

"I'm also doing well." Riley's mom replied to a conversation that Riley could only hear one side of. In almost the same breath, her mom added, "How's your little dog? She's so cute and I hate how nervous she got, I was worried about the poor thing!"

"Lily," Riley whispered. "The dog's name is Lily." Her mom nodded.

"Good, I'm so glad Lily's fine," she said with a wink to Riley. "Yes, Riley's right here, just a moment. It's Mrs. Powell," she whispered as she held her hand over the receiver, "be polite."

Riley forced a smile. Of course she would be polite and she knew it was Mrs. Powell because she was sitting right there! "Hi, Mrs. Powell!"

"Hello, dear. How are you?" The older lady said in her sweet Georgia drawl.

"I'm just fine, how are you?" Riley wouldn't have trouble being polite, but patient. She wanted to ask Mrs. Powell when she could come over already.

"Oh, very well, my dear. I was so happy to get your note in the mail today." Mrs. Powell sounded very pleased indeed. "It seems all I ever get in the mail anymore are credit card applications and political advertisements, neither of which I'm keen to receive, so it was a real treat to get your note. I didn't think young people actually wrote anymore!"

"Oh, I'm so glad. My mom taught me the importance of writing notes." Riley looked at her mom and smiled. She knew her mom would appreciate this comment and as wacky as she could be, Riley loved her very much.

"That's so nice to hear. I was wondering if you would like to join me for tea at my house this Saturday? I know it's short notice and you young people have such busy schedules, but I've kept to myself for several years since James' passing and I would love to have you over. I know little Lily would love to see you, too."

"I'd love to!" Riley said with almost too much enthusiasm. "That would be great," she added as she toned it down a bit after a reproachful look from her mother who was hanging on to every word of their conversation.

"Wonderful! I've always loved afternoon tea, so can you be here at four o'clock?"

"Of course, I'm looking forward to it, thank you!"

"It is my pleasure, Riley. I look forward to planning for your visit," Mrs. Powell said before she hung up the phone.

The minute the phone call was over Riley's mom said, "So... what did she ask you?"

Her mom looked like she was about to jump across the island, seemingly having forgotten about the spaghetti which was about to boil over, so Riley answered quickly. "Mrs. Powell invited me over for afternoon tea on Saturday!" Riley was almost as excited as her mom, though for a very different reason, she couldn't care less about Mrs. Powell's standing in Roswell. Riley cared a lot about finding out what happened to Lily, and after speaking to Mrs. Powell on the phone, Riley was excited to befriend a lonely woman who needed a friend. This made her feel good, and somewhat special that Mrs. Powell would open her home up to her. Riley Carson, a tomboy who loved riding bikes and exploring, over going to the mall and dressing up. Dressing up. Ugh, Riley thought, I'm going to have to dress up. Riley was most comfortable in a t-shirt, jeans, and sneakers, and somehow she thought her mom wasn't going to let her go to afternoon tea with Mrs. Powell wearing her standard "uniform."

As if reading her daughter's mind, her mom said, "I wonder if you have anything appropriate to wear? Perhaps we'll have to go shopping?" Her voice went up an octave, she loved any opportunity to go shopping.

In Riley's mind, worse than having to dress up was going shopping for dress clothes. "Oh, mom, I'm sure I have something I can wear, we don't have to spend any money or anything." Luckily for the Carson girls, money was not an issue, however, unlike her sister, Riley was frugal and certainly didn't want to waste money on some dressy outfit that would never again see the light of day. Hoping to stave off any objection from her mom, Riley added, "I'll look tonight after dinner and show you what I have."

"Okay, but if it doesn't pass the muster, you and I are going shopping Friday night," her mom said as she drained the spaghetti. "Go get your dad and Hailey, dinner's ready!"

Riley was not only glad to make Mrs. Powell happy, she was glad to see how happy her mom was at this moment. She always felt like it was tough to please her mom, something that seemed so natural to Hailey. She knew it was because Hailey and her mom were so alike and Riley was more like her dad, but a girl always wants her mom's approval. As Riley headed to the stairs to call for her sister, she sent a quick text to Finn to let him know about tea on Saturday. She knew he'd be as excited as she was, though her stomach did a flip when she thought about what might happen when she touched Lily again.

# CHAPTER NINETEEN

# *Tea Time*

As Riley predicted, Finn was ecstatic about his best friend's invitation to have afternoon tea with Mrs. Powell, not that he knew what afternoon tea was. Riley filled him in, "It's a fancy tea with sandwiches cut in little triangles and tasty sweets. I'm excited about the food and tea, but really excited to see what I can find out about Lily…and somewhat nervous."

"Are you going to tell Mrs. Powell that we found Lily on the first day of school?"

"I might, I think I'll have to see what happens. Hopefully I can feel what happened to Lily and get more information on where she came from. I'm also just looking forward to getting to know Mrs. Powell. She seems like such a nice lady and it really is cool that she invited me over."

Finn realized they shouldn't only be concerned about the dog and said, "Yeah, all this time we've been so concerned about the dogs, but it really is great that you will also be helping Mrs. Powell. My parents were telling me about the Powells and how long they've been in Roswell. Apparently before her husband died, Mrs. Powell used to go out all the time with him. His death really hurt her and it's so sad to think that she's been alone for some time."

"I know. Can you imagine losing someone who meant that much to you? Someone you spent so much time with?"

"No, they must have really loved each other," Finn said as he quickly glanced at the sidewalk.

"So my mom doesn't think any of my clothes will suffice, so lucky for me, we're going shopping tonight," Riley said with mock excitement and rolled her eyes, smiling at the same time.

"I know how you just love malls."

"Yeah, my favorite place in the world."

"Well, it makes your mom happy, so there's that."

"I know, I just hope we can find something quickly. I really don't want to be in the mall longer than I need to."

Finn laughed at this and said, "You're so funny."

"What?"

"I swear you are more like my mom than your own, and most girls our age for that matter."

"I know, I'm weird, but that's why you like me so much!" Riley gave Finn a good-natured jab in the arm.

"Careful," Finn looked around, "Mrs. Finkelstein might be watching." The two kids busted out laughing as they approached Riley's house.

"Please don't tell me she followed us home?" Riley feigned nervousness as she looked around. "Alright, I better get in there so I can get this shopping over with."

"Have fun!"

"You know it!" Riley bounded up the porch steps. She knew she was lucky to have such a good friend, someone who understood her so well. She hadn't told Finn about her fall into the creek and felt bad she'd held it back. She needed to get up the courage to tell him.

###

Not only did Priscilla buy her youngest daughter a new dress, but she also bought her a new pair of shoes to match. It was Saturday afternoon and Riley was dressed and ready to go…and already hot and uncomfortable. The dress was a heavy emerald green velvet with an itchy collar. Her mom made her wear black tights and her new black patent leather shoes which Riley swore were already cutting off circulation to her pinky toes as she tromped down the stairs.

"Oh, you look beautiful!" Riley's mom squealed with excitement and clasped her cheeks in her hands.

"I'm hot."

"Oh, honey it's just because you've been getting ready. You'll cool down." Riley's mom brushed Riley's brown hair and stuck something in it.

"Wait, what's that?" Riley felt velvety fabric in her hair. She went to the hall mirror to inspect this added accessory. "A flower? A velvet flower? Mom, no." No sooner had she said this than Hailey appeared at the top of the stairs snickering.

"But Riley, it's so…so cute!" Hailey said. She took any opportunity to make fun of her little sister.

"Hailey, leave me alone!" Riley turned on her heel and walked into the kitchen.

Priscilla glared at her oldest daughter. "Hailey, give her a break." She walked into the kitchen where Riley was filling a glass with water, hoping to cool off. She took the velvet flower out of her youngest daughter's hair. "You're right, Roo, no flower. Here, let's try this." Her mom had a thin green velvet headband in her hand. "Just to keep your hair back when you're eating," she said with a gentle smile. Riley's mom placed the accessory in Riley's hair.

Riley nodded, feeling happy that her mom was paying her this kind of attention, the kind normally so foreign for the two of them. She looked at her reflection in the oven and said, "Looks good, and my hair is always tucked behind my ear anyway."

"Great! You look wonderful. Are you ready to go?" Riley's mom wondered if her youngest daughter would ever realize how beautiful she was, inside and out.

Even though Mrs. Powell lived within walking distance, it was a cool day and with these new shoes, Riley wasn't sure she could walk a block without getting blisters all over her feet. "Yep, let's go!" Riley had trouble sleeping the night before as she was so excited about tea with Mrs. Powell. She thought her mom might have had the same problem.

### 

Lucy Mae Powell's home was partially concealed from the street by a large hedge and the old black iron gate on the driveway that was normally closed. The gate was open today and Riley was excited to see Mrs. Powell's home. She passed by this house all the time and always wanted to see the inside. Even though it was hard to see from the street, she could tell it was beautiful. It was an old antebellum home that had survived the Civil War, one of several, and she couldn't wait to see inside.

Mrs. Carson pulled her car slowly up the driveway which was shaded to the right by a large magnolia tree. There were incredible gardens around the home and Riley's mom said, "If these gardens look this good in late Fall, imagine how they'll look in Spring and Summer when everything is in bloom."

The large white house had a deep front porch and columns on three sides. There were two well-worn rocking chairs on the front porch, the floors of which were painted dark green.

Riley's mom parked at the front of the house and marveled at its beauty. "Imagine what this house has seen," she said to Riley who was looking up at the elegant home, craning her neck to see it all. "There's so much history here, Riley, and you are so lucky to have been invited to Mrs. Powell's home."

Riley smiled at her mom who actually sounded real. It wasn't about her, or her getting to meet someone of stature in the community, it was about Riley getting to experience something important due to a connection she had made with a lady who needed a friend. "I know Mom, Mrs. Powell was so nice to invite me over." As she gazed straight ahead, nervously smoothing the velvet on her dress she asked her mom, "What do they call that? It's like a garage but with no walls."

Riley's mom smiled, "It's called a porte-cochere. It's a covered area where carriages could pull up so occupants would be covered if the weather was bad. There's a side entrance to the house there."

"Where do you think Mrs. Powell parks her car then?" Riley asked, simply curious.

Her mom chuckled, "I don't know honey, but it looks like the driveway winds around back, perhaps there's an old barn or newer garage she uses. Let's get going, though, we don't want Mrs. Powell to think you're staying in the car for tea!" Riley's mom checked herself in the mirror, fluffed her hair, and rolled her lips together to make sure her lipstick still looked good, as if she hadn't just done that five minutes before when they left their house. "I'll walk you to the door."

Riley smiled as she opened her door, she knew her mom was excited to get a glimpse of the home as well, and talk to Mrs. Powell again.

"Don't forget the gift!" Riley's mom said as she closed her door.

"Got it!" Riley held a small, but beautifully wrapped gift in her hands. Her mom wrapped it and tied it with a green velvet ribbon that matched Riley's dress. She had to hand it to her mom, she had style and a knack for details.

Riley and her mom walked up the path to the front of the house and up the steps to the porch. "It's even grander from up here." Riley gazed up at the white columns, suddenly feeling very short.

Riley's mom rang the door bell, clearly an update when electricity was added to the home.

Lucy Mae Powell opened the large wooden door and was smartly dressed in trousers and a silk blouse. "Well hello Priscilla, Riley, how are you?"

Riley's mom let her answer, "Great, Mrs. Powell, thank you for inviting me for tea."

"Oh dear, it's my pleasure." Mrs. Powell looked genuinely happy.

"I just wanted to say hello and thank you for your hospitality toward Riley," Priscilla said. "We live close enough that she could walk, but it's a little chilly today." She hugged her camel coat against her.

"Oh yes, it is indeed. Would you like to join us?" Mrs. Powell asked graciously.

Oh no, Riley thought, this is supposed to be my special day.

As if reading her mind, Riley's mom said, "Oh no, thank you, I'm just the chauffeur today." She knew Mrs. Powell was only being polite and only had planned tea for the two of them. "Enjoy the afternoon." She patted her daughter on the back. Poor thing, she thought, feeling that Riley was warm, undoubtedly from a combination of nerves and that velvet dress. Hopefully that house is drafty so she won't be too uncomfortable.

"Lovely seeing you, Priscilla. Riley, won't you come in?" Mrs. Powell said as she and Riley's mom waved goodbye.

While Mrs. Powell's home was large, it was simple because of the time when it was built. There were beautiful hardwood floors and a wide staircase at the back of the foyer. The ceilings were so tall, Riley couldn't help but look up.

"Thirteen feet tall," Mrs. Powell said, noticing Riley admiring her home. "I always like to believe it was thirteen feet for the thirteenth colony," she added, since Georgia was the thirteenth colony of the United States.

"Your home is so pretty."

"Why thank you, dear. It's nice to have some company. It's been lonely since Mr. Powell passed and I'm afraid I've become somewhat of a hermit." Sadness visibly appeared on Mrs. Powell's face and disappeared almost as quickly. "Well, at least it gives the people of Roswell some mystery," she added with a devilish grin and a wink, instantly snapping out of her sadness. "Now, what do you say we have some tea."

"Sounds great." As they entered the sitting room to the left of the foyer, Riley remembered Lily. She looked around but saw no sign of the dog. That's strange, she thought, I would have figured Lily would be right by her side.

"Have a seat, dear," Mrs. Powell gestured to a small table with four chairs and a really pretty lace tablecloth. On the table was a tea set with a pattern of yellow roses, a lovely silver tray of finger sandwiches, and a three tiered serving piece with the prettiest looking desserts.

"Oh, I almost forgot," Riley said handing the pretty square box to Mrs. Powell, "this is for you."

"Why thank you!" Mrs. Powell untied the velvet ribbon and carefully unwrapped the box. Inside was a white tea cup and saucer which Mrs. Powell carefully took out of the box and admired. "Riley, this is beautiful, thank you so much!"

"You're welcome." Riley smiled proudly; she loved giving gifts, mostly to see the happiness it brought people. "It's the lily of the valley pattern for Lily, your dog."

"Oh, that is even more special, thank you."

"There's something else in the box, too."

Mrs. Powell took out some tissue paper and found a package of note cards.

"It's a Maltese, like Lily," Riley said as Mrs. Powell admired the brightly colored note cards which featured a silhouette of a Maltese dog.

"Oh, Riley, thank you so very much. This is the most thoughtful gift." Mrs. Powell set the gifts on the table. "Let's have some tea before it gets cold."

"Is Lily here today?" Riley asked with a little apprehension as Mrs. Powell poured tea into the delicate cups. She was surprised she hadn't been greeted by the dog already.

"Oh yes, she's out back. I've got the mobile groomer here giving her a bath. She was supposed to be here earlier, but got delayed, but don't worry, she'll be done soon. Lily isn't fond of baths, in fact, when she was rescued, it looked like she had never even had a bath before, according to the rescue group. It's much easier if I get a little assistance with that and it's easier on Lily."

"Oh, great!" Riley took a sip of hot tea, she was glad she took Mrs. Powell's suggestion to have it with milk and honey.

Mrs. Powell picked up a small triangular sandwich filled with egg salad. "These are my favorite."

"Mrs. Powell, have you lived in Roswell all your life?" Riley asked.

"Yes, dear, I have. My family was one of the founding families of Roswell, so our roots go deep here. I just love this city. Of course it has changed a lot since I was your age."

"What was it like?"

"Oh, it was much simpler and slower-paced. Of course I'm sure we got up to the same kinds of things you and your friends do today. We rode bicycles around town, fished in Vickery Creek, scouted for adventure all summer long."

"Adventure? What kind of adventure?"

"Well, you know that this was Cherokee Indian land, right?" Mrs. Powell asked as she took a sip of tea.

"Yes, ma'am."

"Thousands of Cherokee were among those who had lived here and were forced out on the Trail of Tears. Some stayed, those who wished to assimilate, but they lost their land as it was sold to white people who wanted to settle here, my family included." Mrs. Powell said with regret even though she had nothing to do with it. "However, my family and many others in the area, worked and lived with the Indians who stayed behind and they got on quite peacefully."

"Wasn't there enough land for everyone?" Riley asked.

"Plenty, of course, but when gold was discovered on Cherokee land in Dahlonega, the state had an agreement with the federal government to declare the Cherokee Nation illegal and their land was divided up and sold to white settlers in a land lottery.

"We were talking about this at dinner one night. Why did some of the Cherokee stay and some leave?"

"Well dear, the Cherokee tribe was split. You can imagine how you would feel if your land was suddenly given to someone else by the government. Some of the Cherokee wanted to stay here and assimilate, even if it meant losing their land, while others couldn't stand for that. It's a very complicated issue and I could go on for hours." Mrs. Powell didn't seem upset, but she was trying to be diplomatic and stay away from such discussions while entertaining. "Anyway, I was telling you about our adventures." She was excited to talk about her younger years. "We would go looking for arrowheads and other artifacts that were left behind by the Indians and did find some by Vickery Creek and the Chattahoochee River."

"That's so cool! We haven't found anything like that." She didn't want to tell Mrs. Powell about what she and her friends had found at the creek.

"It was very neat to find artifacts like that. You can see some of them at the Visitor's Center across from the Square. There was one thing that we never could find, though."

"What's that?" Riley shifted forward in her chair, eager to find out.

"There's a legend that there are caves between Vickery Creek and the Chattahoochee River and that some of the Cherokee who stayed behind lived in the caves. Some say they had found gold of their own and hid it in the caves. There were all sorts of stories, about the caves being booby-trapped so the gold would stay safe, that the Cherokee put a curse on the caves, you know how these stories develop over time, they get grander and grander as the years go by!" Mrs. Powell's eyes lit up with excitement.

"My dad told me about the caves! He grew up here too and said he looked for them, but never found them either."

"No, we never did find those caves." Mrs. Powell dabbed at the corner of her mouth with a monogrammed linen napkin. "Well, we found *a* cave, but it wasn't *the* cave."

"How do you know?" Riley grabbed a shortbread cookie, intent on hearing anything Mrs. Powell had to say about her adventures in their town.

"Well, I'm not certain it wasn't the cave of the legend, but it was a small cave, not at all as described in the stories. In the stories it sounded like a cave system, like a labyrinth. When my husband, James, and I were kids, we used to go looking for the caves. Back then, the area was much different and the terrain much wilder and more treacherous. James thought there had been a cave-in at the back of the cave we found, but it was hard to tell and much too dangerous to explore. In any case, there wasn't anything hidden in it, no evidence of old booby-traps or treasure found, just a small, empty cave."

"I suppose I wondered if the stories were really true, or just legends passed down from generation to generation. James, he was a lover of fantasy, and he talked about those caves even up to his passing. He was sure they were out there, he even kept a journal when we were kids and drew maps of what he thought it would look like based on the stories he had gathered from older friends and relatives. He was a wonderful man, indeed." Mrs. Powell now dabbed at the corner of her eye with her napkin.

"Do you still have his journal?"

"Oh, I'm sure it's here somewhere." Mrs. Powell said as she looked around her large home. "I did recently donate several of his books, though, sometimes the memories are just too hard."

"I'm sorry." Riley was upset with herself for saying anything that would have brought up sad memories for Mrs. Powell.

"Oh dear, I'm the one who should apologize for getting all weepy on you," Mrs. Powell said with a bright smile. "It sure has been nice having your company. I guess I've turned into a blabbermouth since I've been alone for so long. It's nice to have someone other than Lily to talk to." They both laughed as a knock sounded at the back door.

"Speaking of the little devil, I bet she's all done with her grooming. Excuse me, dear." Mrs. Powell lifted her small, but strong frame from her chair and set off to the back of the house.

Riley's heart began to pound. She had been so interested in listening to Mrs. Powell and the story about the caves, she had almost forgotten about Lily! Riley heard Mrs. Powell open the heavy, squeaky door and then heard little feet clicking quickly across the old wooden floors. A little white ball of fur came flying into the room, then out of the room, then back into the room, up on the settee, then around the settee. Lily stopped abruptly, lowered her chest to the floor, her bottom and tail in the air, and looked at Riley. Riley knew this was called a "play bow" which meant Lily wanted to play. Riley got up from the table and knelt across from Lily, about four feet from her. "Hey, Lily. Come here." Riley patted the top of her knees.

Lily's tail began to wag slowly from side to side and she sprinted to Riley and promptly rolled over, showing Riley her pink belly. "That's a good girl," Riley said as she scratched Lily's chest. She immediately felt a jolt of electricity. Riley felt darkness and hunger. It was dark and scary, and it was damp. A tall, dark figure came toward the dog and Riley was overwhelmed by sounds of whimpering from all around. The figure grabbed the dog by the scruff of its neck. The dog was thrown against something hard, a wall? Pain. Riley felt pain in her head and neck, throbbing. She felt dizzy, disoriented, sick to her stomach. The tall figure raised something in the air. The figure has a weird head. A hat, the figure is wearing a hat of some kind. Panic, survival, this is what Riley felt now. The dog took off running, stumbling, but running hard, scared. It was a fear Riley has never experienced before. She couldn't catch her breath, and she was burning up.

"Riley! Are you okay, dear?" Mrs. Powell came rushing to Riley's side.

Lily hopped up and greeted her mama as Riley snapped back to reality. "Yes, ma'am. I'm fine," she said as she touched her forehead which was throbbing. "I was just thinking about Lily and…well, I just can't imagine who could have treated her so badly." Riley tried to compose herself so she didn't scare Mrs. Powell.

"I know, dear. Evil exists in this world, even in our fine town. It's our job to fight evil and be good citizens, to be good examples to those around us." Mrs. Powell put the back of her hand against Riley's forehead. "Honey, you are so hot and you've lost your color, are you sure you're okay?"

"Yes, ma'am. I think it's this stupid dress, the velvet makes me so hot," Riley fibbed as she got to her feet.

"Well, you look lovely, but next time you just come as you are, no need for fancy dress around here. Honestly, I prefer it that way myself," Mrs. Powell said with a cheerful smile. "Here, have a sip of water." She handed Riley a water glass with a slice of lemon floating on the top. "All this hot tea and that velvet dress is making you hot."

"Thanks, Mrs. Powell." Riley was grateful for the cool water which did make her feel better.

"Why don't we get some fresh air, dear?" Mrs. Powell thought the cool air would help Riley. "I'm sure Lily needs a potty break and I'd love to show you around the garden."

"That would be great." Riley was happy to get out into the cool evening.

Mrs. Powell put Lily on her pink leash and they headed out the side door where the porte-cochere was and to the back garden. Riley saw that the driveway continued to a more modern garage on the other side of the house. Mrs. Powell was telling Riley what the dormant plants were and how pretty they would look in spring and summer. "You must visit me when these are all in bloom. We could have tea in the garden," Mrs. Powell said hopefully.

"That would be wonderful, I love flowers and would love to see your garden when everything is in bloom!" Riley said as Lily finally decided on a place to do her business after much investigating.

"Wonderful. It's a date!"

As they headed back inside, Riley thought that Mrs. Powell seemed happy and was glad that she was making a new friend with her. She was feeling better now that she had fresh air. She loved Lily but was now scared to touch her again since the sensation had been so powerful. She wondered if Lily had communicated everything she needed to, she also wondered if this so-called "gift" was becoming a curse. She didn't want to be afraid to touch a dog, she loved dogs!

Just then the doorbell rang and Lily ran to the front door, barking her little head off. "See, she's a good watch dog, too." Mrs. Powell looked at her watch. "That must be your mom."

"Thank you so much for inviting me over, Mrs. Powell." Riley and her new friend headed to the foyer. "I had such a great time."

"It's my pleasure, dear. Anytime you want to drop by, you are more than welcome. Your friends, too." Mrs. Powell scooped her barking dog into her arms. "I enjoy having company now, it's been too long."

Mrs. Powell opened the door where Riley's mom was waiting, her face beaming. "Hi! Did y'all have a nice time?"

"Yes we did. You've got quite a wonderful young lady here.

She's welcome back any time, but going forward, dress code is casual around here," she said with a genuine smile to Riley.

"She's my little sweetheart!" Riley's mom said with pride.

"Thanks again, Mrs. Powell," Riley said as Mrs. Powell hugged her with her free arm, Lily occupying her other arm. Riley tentatively reached out to Lily who licked her fingers. She scratched Lily's fine hair on the top of her head and the little dog seemed to beam with happiness. Nothing, good, Riley thought. Lily showed me all she needed to.

"Thank you for spending your afternoon with me, dear," Mrs. Powell said. "See you soon!"

"See you soon!" Riley practically skipped off the porch. She couldn't wait to tell Finn about today, but first she couldn't wait to get out of this hot, itchy dress! Riley was normally not a fan of the cold weather, but the cold air felt good right now. She knew it wasn't just the dress that had made her so hot, she couldn't believe how much she had seen when she petted Lily. She needed to talk to Finn while the experience was still fresh in her mind.

# CHAPTER TWENTY

## *Still Searching*

Riley's mom was so excited about and interested in her daughter's time with Lucy Mae Powell that she peppered Riley with questions the whole, albeit short, drive home. What was her house like? Is it beautiful? Did you see the back garden? What was she like? What did she serve? What did she serve it in? And on it went. Riley was grateful that the ride home was a quick one, she even unfastened her seatbelt before the car had pulled into the garage.

"Mom, this dress is hot and itchy, I gotta go change," Riley said as her mom continued to ask questions after she had turned off the car, "and I gotta call Finn."

"Okay, sweetie, we'll talk later," Riley's mom called up to her daughter who had taken off her shoes and was taking the steps two at a time, headed toward her bedroom.

Riley quickly changed out of her stuffy clothes and called Finn, filling him in on every last detail from the caves to the experience with Lily.

"Wow! She knows about the caves, too? That's so cool!" Finn's excitement was evident over the phone. In fact, he seemed more excited about the caves than what Riley learned from Lily. "And Hailey thought it was all just a myth!"

"I know, that's what I thought! What about my experience with Lily, though? It doesn't give us too many clues."

"Well, did the tall figure look male or female?" Finn asked.

"Male."

"Was he fat, thin, average?"

"He was thin, I think." Riley thought back to the horrifying sensations of fear and pain. She closed her eyes and winced, "Yeah, thin. I could only see his silhouette, so I don't know what ethnicity he was or what his features looked like, but I think he wore some sort of hat. Wherever they were, it was really dark, damp, and smelly. And Finn, I think there are lots of dogs. I heard so many it was deafening."

"Oh gosh, that's awful," Finn said. "Who knows, it could be someone who lives right under our noses, but has something creepy going on in his basement."

"That's a scary thought." Riley was trying to shake the images she had seen. "What are you up to tomorrow?"

"My dad and I are going fishing in North Georgia."

"Oh, that's right. Darn, I was hoping we could try to figure this out. I'll see if I can figure out anything on my own tomorrow, try to put the pieces together."

"Okay, cool. Maybe we should look at a map and see if we can make any sense out of where these dogs were found and what's nearby, buildings, homes…I know we know where they were found, but maybe if we mark it out, something will clue us in." Finn felt like he didn't have much to offer about the one thing they were trying to figure out.

"That's a good idea." Riley was feeling a little hopeless, too.

"Let's go to the library during lunch break. No one will be in there and hey, maybe Mrs. Willnow will know something about those caves." Finn was clearly unable to let go of this additional adventure. "If they exist, maybe they're haunted!"

"Okay, but I don't want us to lose sight of figuring out what's happening to these dogs. Don't you think it's weird that no one has claimed that their dogs are missing?" Riley was hoping to get Finn back on track.

"Good point. I'll think about that some more tonight. That's a really good point…"

"Okay, have a good night, see you Monday."

"You, too, bye!"

No one has claimed their dogs are missing, Riley thought about this more. That doesn't make a lot of sense. But then again, these dogs were in pretty bad shape, so if they aren't taking care of them, they would get in trouble if they claimed them as their own. Her mind was racing so she got out her journal. She smoothed her hand over the leather cover and thought about Mr. Powell's journals and the stories they could tell. Looking at her journal reminded her of other journals she had seen. When she had detention at the library, she cataloged journals for Mrs. Willnow! She would email her in hopes that they were Mr. Powell's journals. Maybe Mrs. Powell had donated them after all! She opened her journal where the ribbon marker was and started writing about her day. She wrote about everything; tea with Mrs. Powell, what Lily showed her, the caves. Every thought, detail, and possible scenario. Writing it all down helped calm her mind and this would help her remember everything. As she wrote, she couldn't help but think there was something familiar about the figure she saw.

###

After church on Sunday, Riley spent most of the day researching; everything from caves in Roswell, of which she found very little information, to the psychology of someone who abuses dogs. She was pretty tired by the time dinner rolled around and was grateful to hear her dad's voice calling her downstairs. She was ready to eat dinner, watch some TV with her family, and see if Finn had any theories when she saw him the next day.

When she got downstairs, her dad looked at her with concern and said, "Roo, is everything okay? You look pretty stressed for a Sunday evening."

"Oh, I'm fine dad, just getting some work done," Riley half-fibbed. Her parents didn't know anything about her ability to "feel" what the dogs had experienced, or her concerns about what could be happening in their fair city. Besides, they always told her she had such an imagination…She knew something was going on here and needed to figure it out. She decided to explore a lighter topic. "Dad, did you know that the Powells found a cave in Roswell?"

"Yeah, I heard they found a cave when they were young," her dad said as he made a shallow pool in his mashed potatoes with the back of his spoon and grabbed the gravy boat, "but it was a small cave with only one chamber. The cave system described in the stories would have been much, much larger. Large enough to house Native Americans and hide their gold," he said with a wink.

"Do you think the Cherokee booby-trapped the caves or put a curse on them?" Riley asked as she sat straight up in her chair, excited about the prospect of this being true.

"Well, if I had hidden gold, I probably would have boo-by-trapped it!"

"Do you know where the cave that the Powells found is?" Riley hoped her dad had some insight.

"Well, I know that the land they found it on is now part of the National Park in between the Chattahoochee River and Vickery Creek, but that's a large expanse of terrain that is quite steep in places. Some areas it's a sheer drop-off toward the river. We used to look for it when we were younger, but we never found anything. Then as I got older, I was more interested in hanging out on the banks of the creek as girls sunbathed nearby." Riley's dad winked at her mom this time.

"Oh, Jack, the girls don't want to hear that!"

"Well, I was just waiting for you to come along, sweetheart," he said as he reached for his wife's hand.

Riley was enjoying the light-hearted mood her parents seemed to be in; it was refreshing and it took her mind off the stress of trying to figure out what was happening to the dogs. Maybe she was thinking about it too much? Maybe she needed a good diversion like the caves? She thought she should take Finn's earlier advice and step away from the problem in hopes that she could see it more clearly. She thought about the caves and whether or not they could be near Old Mill Park. The instant she thought of the park, she recalled her last experience there and got chills. She had avoided telling Finn about what had happened, but knew she needed to tell him about it. She couldn't shake the image of the man who saved her. Maybe Finn could help her figure out what it all meant.

# CHAPTER TWENTY-ONE

## *Enchanted Land*

At school on Monday, Riley was excited to meet Finn and Eve at lunch to see what they could figure out. Just as the trio were headed into the library, Corey Thornton saw them and said, "Hey nerds, why are you going to the library on lunch break? Can't you afford a computer?" Seth and Brad were snickering on either side of him. "Oh, that's right, your friend Eve probably can't, after all her dad's just a cop!"

Finn moved toward Corey, fed up with his constant comments and just as he was about to open his mouth, Mrs. Finkelstein rounded the corner.

"Students in the hallway? Where are you supposed to be?" Mrs. Finkelstein asked.

"I was just heading to the cafeteria when-" Corey said.

"It's okay, Mrs. F! I've got this covered," Mrs. Willnow bellowed from the doorway of the library and looked particularly stern. "Finn, Riley, Eve, in here, now." She extended her arm out pointing them in the direction of the library.

Riley's stomach did a flip. She wondered, is she really mad at us? She headed into the deserted library and tucked her hair behind her ear.

As Finn and Eve followed behind Riley, Mrs. Willnow was on their heels. "Come. Follow me." She walked ahead of them and to the back corner of the library toward her office, marching at a quick clip.

Riley looked back at Finn and Eve, her two friends looking as worried as she felt. Finn shrugged.

"Here. Sit." Mrs. Willnow pointed to a work table just outside her office. She turned around with a gigantic grin across her face and said, "Saved you from her, huh?"

Riley exhaled, "I thought you were mad at us!"

"Mad? Heavens no! I had to pretend, though, didn't I? While I do enjoy your company in here, I don't think your parents would like you getting detention again, *young ladies,*" she said the last two words mimicking Mrs. Finkelstein.

Finn was grinning from ear to ear, "You should be the drama coach, Mrs. Willnow!"

"Now, let's not get carried away," she said with a wink. "Here, I wanted to show you something." The librarian pulled out a couple of old journals and what looked like Georgia history books. "Riley emailed me yesterday about researching local geography around the Chattahoochee River and I think I've found something."

"Have you heard the stories about the caves?" Eve asked her.

"No, dear. I'm not much into geography, but Riley seemed keen to find out more, so I found these old books and journals I bought at an estate sale over the summer."

Mrs. Willnow was moving quickly today, Riley thought she seemed preoccupied.

"The books are old Georgia History and Geography books, so I thought they'd come in handy. These journals date back to the mid-1900's and were part of an estate sale, I can't recall whose. I love old books and journals and recall picking these up because there were some really great drawings in here. I think you'd appreciate them," Mrs. Willnow said to Riley as she slid the journals over to her and started toward her office. "I've got a lot to do, so I'm going to leave you with these so you can see if there's anything of interest to you. There are some notes in the journals about caves, but not too much detail. Honestly I thought you'd appreciate the drawings, lots of wildlife drawings, some beautiful ones of birds."

"Thanks, Mrs. Willnow." Riley carefully picked up a journal and began to flip through it.

Eve scanned the index of the book on Georgia history, looking for something about the Cherokee and the area around the Chattahoochee as Riley and Finn looked through the journals.

"A map!" Finn had just turned to a page near the back of the journal.

"Wow!" Riley's eyes were wide as she took in the hand-drawn map. "It's faint in some places, but over all it's in good shape."

"So this drawing is kinda crude, but, I think the thin line winding down from the top of the page is Vickery Creek and the thick line at the bottom is the Chattahoochee River." Finn traced the lines on the page. The drawing also showed a circle with lines intersecting, like a pizza cut in pieces, and directly off of that was a rectangle that was on top of the thin line. Off to the far side of the page was a thick black 'X' mark.

"What's that?" Eve pointed to the pizza-looking object.

Finn thought for a moment about the area and the terrain, "The mill!"

Riley scooted closer to look. "Yeah, so the section where the 'X' is…"

"Is Old Mill Park!" The three friends said this almost in unison.

"That confirms what my dad said! He said that the Powells found a small cave in the area between the creek and the river that is now part of the Chattahoochee National Park," Riley was talking at double-speed.

"Do you think this is it?" Eve asked.

"Well, he said the cave they found was not large enough to be the cave system from the legend. It was only one chamber, not a whole system of large caves."

Finn pointed to the drawing again, "Well, this drawing shows a location, but no detail, so we can't be sure of what this is." He flipped through the pages written before and after the map was drawn. "I'll see if there's any mention of the caves."

Riley flipped through the other journal and said, "If I was writing about something I wanted kept secret, I wouldn't be too obvious in my journal."

"Yeah, good point." Eve randomly flipped through the Geography book.

"There are some great drawings in here," Riley said, "This cardinal is beautiful."

Eve said, "You know, they say when you see a cardinal that it's a loved one coming back to visit you."

"That's cool." Riley immediately thought of Sammy.

"Look, I don't mean to ruin your moment, but caves, let's focus on the caves." Finn had a wry grin on his face and Riley and Eve giggled at him.

Eve looked at the clock on the wall, "Yeah we don't have much longer."

Riley continued to flip through the journal she had. "Look! Here's a similar drawing but where the 'X' was, are these little odd-shaped circles." Finn and Eve put their books down and scooted close to Riley. Again there was a thin line coming from the top of the page and a thicker line across the bottom of the page. The two lines joined on the lower left of the page. There was a cluster of shapes in between the lines, off to the far right, opposite from where the two lines met. The page title said, 'Enchanted Land.'

"What do you suppose the title means?" Eve asked.

"I don't know, but let's look it up later," Riley said.

"Okay, so this means that if this is Vickery Creek…" Finn traced the thin line with his finger from where it joined the thick line, "…then if these are the caves, they are to the East and North of where it joins with the Chattahoochee."

Eve had a confused look on her face and Riley turned the book around. "So, if this is the entrance to Old Mill Park, and around here is the covered bridge, then the caves should be over here."

"Oh yeah, I see now!" Eve said, "but that's a lot of ground to cover."

"Yeah, these clearly aren't drawn to scale," Finn said.

Riley snapped pictures of the pages with the maps and other pages in the journal that interested her. "Clearly we're going to have to do some research."

"We should probably go eat while we still have time." Eve closed the book she had been looking through.

Finn had gone back to his journal and was quickly scanning the pages, "Just give me a sec…"

Riley and Eve stacked up all the books while Finn was looking at the journal. "Here, a few pages before the map in this journal it says, 'I've heard stories of caves, so I think I'll take a hike and see if I can find anything. I've always loved adventure.'"

"How do we even know that these drawings are giving the location of the caves?" Eve asked.

"We don't, but we can always go look there." Finn closed the journal and placed it on the top of the stack that Riley was holding, ready to give the books back to Mrs. Willnow. He smiled, "After all, I've always loved adventure!"

# CHAPTER TWENTY-TWO

## Mister Oscar

Saturday finally arrived and Finn and Riley went to Eve's house to discuss the location of the Cherokee caves. As Riley and Finn walked up the old brick path to Eve's house, her brother Evan was walking to his truck. "Hey guys!" He said with a wave.

"Hi!" Riley said smiling brightly.

"Hey, Evan," Finn said.

"You staying out of trouble?" Evan looked right at Riley.

"Uh…," Finn started, then realized Evan was talking to Riley.

"Of course." Riley tucked her hair behind her ear as Finn looked at her with a questioning glance.

"Good, see you later." Evan got into his Bronco and the loud engine roared.

"What was that all about?" Finn asked.

"I'm sure it was just a figure of speech. You know, small talk," Riley said though Finn wasn't buying it.

Eve greeted her friends at the door, they said hello to Mr. Rycroft, and grabbed a snack from the kitchen before heading upstairs to Eve's room. Eve's small room was organized to make the most of the space. She had a daybed against the right wall which left plenty of room for a good-sized desk in front of the windows which also featured a built-in reading nook. There was enough space for the three of them to sit around the desk and lay out their materials. "I printed this map," Eve indicated to a large map laid out on the table. It was an actual map of the area around Old Mill Park printed on copy paper and carefully taped together to make sure it met at all the right places.

"Wow, this is great!" Finn said.

"Yeah, so much easier than trying to look at the map on one of our computer screens," Riley said.

"Here, each of us should mark where we think the caves are. While we have the drawing, it doesn't really help us figure out the exact spot." Eve handed Riley a green colored pencil, gave Finn the blue, and kept the purple for herself.

The three friends plotted where they thought the caves could be and explained why they picked these places. Most of their spots were picked for geographic reasons due to the terrain and position near the water, and some of their spots were close to one another.

"Here, I want to show you something," Eve opened her laptop. "I was researching the caves and Roswell history and I found some interesting information. It's kinda hard to find much more about the Cherokee in this area, other than what we already knew. I had to dig and dig, but I found this."

Riley and Finn looked at the page and started reading where Eve pointed. Finn read aloud, "Many believe that the Cherokee found gold in areas close to the Chattahoochee River and hid it in caves near Vickery Creek."

"Wow, that's awesome!" Riley's eyes lit up.

"Yeah, but it doesn't say much more," Finn said. "It's like we keep hearing this, but don't get any confirmation."

"I guess if gold was hidden, it's not a good idea to broadcast it to the world," Eve said.

"Yeah, besides, it's been so long, I'm sure if it was hidden it's likely it has already been found," Finn said.

"Something that was easy to find was the reference to *Enchanted Land*." Riley opened her small notebook. "A quick search brought up several pages about Roswell. 'Enchanted Land' was what the Cherokee called the area that is now Roswell."

"That's so cool!" Finn said.

"It's definitely a special place," Eve said.

"So, if that one map was labeled 'Enchanted Land', that references the Cherokee and Roswell! I bet the drawings depict where the caves are." Finn was really excited and was searching another page about Roswell, trying to find out more information.

"The gold may be gone, but it would be kinda neat to say we found the caves," Riley said.

"Yeah, but don't forget what we're dealing with," Eve motioned to the map laid out in front of them, "this area is huge."

"Yeah, finding these caves may be harder than finding Lily was," Riley said as Finn continued to scroll through a website which had lots of old photos of Roswell.

"Wait, stop!" Riley said, "scroll back up."

Finn scrolled the mouse to reveal an old photo.

"It can't be…" Riley said.

"What?" Finn asked.

"This man, I've met him," Riley said pointing to a man in

the picture.

"What? You couldn't have met him, this photo was taken in 1860." Finn pointed to the caption and looked at Riley whose face had gone pale. "He was a slave who lived at Bulloch Hall."

"Yes, she could have," Eve said. "He's been watching over us."

"What? How?" Finn was now thoroughly confused.

"He's…a ghost. He's been watching over us since we've been investigating. He thinks we're crazy, but he wants to keep us safe, so he stays near us," Eve said.

"Why haven't you said anything before now?" Riley asked.

"Because…even though I know you said you don't think I'm crazy, sometimes I just feel weird about it. I mean, it's not normal."

"No, it's not normal, it's a gift." Riley thought of her own ability and thought, I'm sure it can feel like a curse.

"But, *you've* seen him?" Finn looked at Riley. "When? And why didn't you tell me, I mean us?" Finn now looked at Eve, "He's been around us?"

"Yeah, remember when we got off the swing set at Sloan Street Park and the third swing was swinging on its own?" Eve asked Finn who nodded. "That was Mister Oscar."

"Mister Oscar? Cool!" Finn said. "Why didn't you say anything then?"

"Because I wanted to get to the creek before dark, and if I said something, I knew you two would want to investigate. Plus, he's been around a few more times, watching over us. I figured he would present himself to you if he wanted to."

Riley could sense that she'd hurt her best friend's feelings and felt horrible for not telling him sooner. "Finn, I didn't say anything because I wasn't even sure what happened, and honestly, I tried to forget about it."

Finn's voice grew serious, "What do you mean? What happened?"

Riley told Finn and Eve all about her fall into Vickery Creek and the man who saved her. "It just happened, and I didn't tell you because it was scary. Not seeing him. I mean seeing him was weird, but I think he saved my life."

"Wow, that's amazing," Eve said.

"Yeah, amazingly stupid," Riley said. "I shouldn't have gone there by myself and shouldn't have gone off the trail like I did."

"You could have died! I can't believe you didn't tell me!" Finn threw his pencil on the table, he was simultaneously angry and relieved. He stood up, took a deep breath and ran his hand through his hair. "Thank goodness Mr. Oscar was there."

"I think he's an angel," Riley said, relieved to have told her friends what happened.

"Your EVP!" Eve said.

Finn looked at Riley. "Oh my gosh, do you think that was Mister Oscar?"

Riley thought about it. "The voice on the EVP was so quiet, and when I was pulled from the creek, I could hear him like I can hear you two right now." She closed her eyes and thought about it, "I can't be sure, but it could be. I mean, he was warning us, then he...saved me."

Finn didn't want to say anything, especially in front of Eve, but he was pretty shaken up by Riley's story. He didn't know what he would do if he lost his best friend and was really upset that she didn't tell him about it sooner. "I need a break, I'm going to go get some water." He grabbed his half-full glass and headed downstairs.

### 

Finn was stunned about what Riley had just told them. Why didn't she tell me? He thought. Finn couldn't believe Riley hadn't told him right away, but was glad she was okay. Maybe she didn't know whether to believe it herself, he thought. He got more water, drank it down then got some more, pausing in the kitchen to think about all he'd just heard. As he headed back upstairs, he heard Mr. Rycroft on the phone in his study off the hallway.

"Glen, this is getting scary. We've now accounted for six dogs that all look like they have been abused or neglected. We can't let the press find out; we've got to solve this before they hear about it," Mr. Rycroft said into the phone.

After a pause, Mr. Rycroft said, "I have a few places I'd like to check out, let's meet at the station in an hour to talk about this."

Finn used the hallway mirror to see into the study. Mr. Rycroft was jotting something down on a pad of paper.

"Okay, sounds good, Glen. See you in a few," Mr. Rycroft said as he hung up the phone.

Finn quickly yet quietly headed back upstairs with his water. When he got into Eve's room, he shut the door and told his friends what he just overheard.

"Oh my gosh, six dogs?" Eve asked.

"That's awful, but I'm afraid there might be more." Riley

felt sick to her stomach, thinking back to touching Lily and all the whimpering she heard.

"I wonder what places my dad wants to check out?" Eve asked.

"I have an idea," Finn said.

The three kids had quickly ended their search for the caves and the legend of the Cherokee gold and were back to discussing the dogs. Six dogs was a lot. Something was definitely going on. After a half an hour, Mr. Rycroft came upstairs to let the kids know he was heading out, but that Evan was on his way home. Before Evan got home, the kids ran down to the study. Finn found the pad Mr. Rycroft had used and grabbed a pencil off a cup on the desk. He began lightly rubbing the pencil across the pad. Ever so slightly, they could read the three places Mr. Rycroft wanted to check out:

Allenbrook House

Creepy House

Mill Ruins

The kids took the list upstairs to talk so they wouldn't be interrupted by Evan when he got home.

"Ri, you said when you laid hands on Mrs. Powell's dog, it was dark and damp. Do you think there were windows?" Finn asked.

Riley closed her eyes trying to visualize the scene. "No, it was completely dark, no light."

"We know the Creepy House is on a crawl space," Eve suggested, referring to the old gray house on the famous Roswell Ghost Walk that had several extremely creepy stories surrounding it.

"Too small," Riley said. "And too close to Atlanta Street. I would have heard the traffic."

"And with that many dogs, the area around the Creepy House is too busy. Someone would have heard their barking." Finn crossed out the Creepy House.

"The Allenbrook House was recently renovated and the National Park Service owns it," Eve said after a quick search online. "My dad must have it on his list for a reason, but I doubt the dogs are being kept there."

"Yeah, that wouldn't make any sense, people work there." Finn crossed it off the list.

"The Mill Ruins don't make sense either," Riley said. "There aren't any real structures left where dogs could be kept. What I saw was a dark, dank place. All the ruins are in the open." She seemed deflated. This list didn't make sense with what she saw.

"Maybe he means the two-story brick building right next to the creek and the covered bridge." Eve suggested, trying to help her dad out. "I think that building was the machine shop for the mill."

"Again that building is right in the middle of everything, someone would have heard dogs," Finn said.

"Yeah, you're right," Eve said, now she was feeling discouraged.

"Hang on!" Finn said as he felt along the bottom of the paper. "There's something else here." He grabbed the pencil and started lightly rubbing across the bottom of the page, moving close to the page to see what it said

There were two words: Cherokee Caves??

The three friends looked at each other in amazement.

"Maybe they really do exist!" Riley felt a renewed optimism.

"Yeah, my dad wouldn't even consider something if he thought it was just a legend," Eve said.

Finn cleared off the desk revealing the map they were working with earlier. "Let's decide which area makes the most sense for these caves. We'll take our best shot."

"Well," Eve pointed to the map, "it looks like this area is one spot where you both plotted points not far from each other. It's also closest to where we found the dog that disappeared after we got my dad."

"What do we have to lose?" Finn said, "It is the most logical place."

"Let's start there, then!" Riley said.

Eve looked bummed, "There's no way Evan will let me go out without my dad's permission."

"Okay," Riley said, "keep your phone near you in case we run into trouble. You can help us if we get in a bind or need some more information."

"You got it," Eve had a look of worry in her eyes. "Please be safe."

"We will." Finn looked at Riley, "You good with this?"

"I wouldn't let you go alone. Let's just remember what Mister Oscar said." Riley tucked her hair behind her ear. "Hopefully he'll come along for the ride." She sounded more brave than she felt at that moment.

# CHAPTER TWENTY-THREE

## *Cave Hunting*

Riley and Finn crossed the covered bridge and headed up the steep concrete steps that led to the upper trail. "Finn?" Riley said.

"Yeah?"

"If we find more dogs, we might also find the person or people who are mistreating them."

"I know. We need to be careful. I want to find the dogs, if there are more, but if we think we're in trouble, we'll call Mr. Rycroft."

Riley felt the hair on the back of her neck stand up and immediately thought of their guardian angel, Mister Oscar. "I hope Mister Oscar is with us," she said as they reached the top of the hill.

"So you really were saved by a ghost, huh?"

"I guess so. He looked just like that man in the picture, Mister Oscar. Finn…I was having trouble keeping my head above the water, the current was so swift. I may not be able to explain it, but he saved me."

"That's amazing…I'm so glad he did." Finn didn't want to think of what could have happened had Mister Oscar not been there. "While we're out here, we may as well do some ghost hunting. Maybe Mister Oscar will say 'hi'." He pulled out his mini recorder and EMF meter which he seemed to always have stowed in his pockets, just in case. Riley swore that's why he loved cargo pants and shorts, so he could carry all his stuff wherever he went.

Riley took out the map Eve had printed for them of the section of the park that they guessed might be concealing the Cherokee Caves. "It looks like we need to head East on the trail and we'll come to a clearing where we will need to get off the trail."

It was about 2:00 and there was plenty of afternoon light. It was a nice late autumn day, but a bit on the brisk side. It seemed that most of the hikers were finishing up their treks, having planned to be outside during the warmest part of the day. As the two friends hiked the trail, they were fairly quiet, Finn working with his EMF meter. He knew they were both on edge, so he had suggested the ghost hunting.

"Is anyone out here with us?" Riley said into the open space around them.

Finn paused before asking the next question, "Mister Oscar, are you here with us?"

They waited and heard nothing, knowing that even though they didn't hear anything, they may be recording audio that the naked ear could not hear.

"Are there any Native Americans here?" Riley said.

Again, after another pause, Finn asked, "Are there any Cherokee here?" He gave Riley a wink.

After leaving time for a response, Riley said, "Yeah, I guess they didn't call themselves Native Americans back then." She was smiling now and felt a bit more at ease.

As the two neared the clearing where they would turn off

the path, they studied the map again. After they decided in which direction they would head, Finn took a small piece of plastic ribbon out of his pocket, the kind they use when marking which trees not to cut down in a new development.

"I'm going to tie this to this sapling here, that way we know where to go when we're coming back. I'll tie them along our route so we can find our way, and since these are used for marking trees anyway, hopefully they won't look suspicious." Finn was always three steps ahead in planning.

"How in the world did you know we'd be doing this today?"

Finn was sort of fanatical about being prepared which came from his dad. "Well, after the time we found the dog and went to get Mr. Rycroft, I realized if we kept looking around here and needed to go deeper in the forest, we'd need something better than chalk. Just look around here. Now that the leaves have fallen, this is a vast area of browns and tans, of course with the leaves off the trees and many plants dormant, at least we can see a good distance, but this is some thick forest, especially when we go off the trail."

"I'm glad you're always so prepared." Riley was seriously grateful that her friend was so clever.

Finn traded his ghost hunting tools for his compass as the two headed through the clearing and into dense woods. "Somewhere in these woods, we should notice an elevation, and on the south side should be the caves." Finn tied another tree where the woods began and the two headed in, crunching on top of all the dead leaves.

"Well, if someone is here, we sure aren't going to sneak up on them," Riley said as a nervousness filled her stomach.

Finn knew she was right and said a little prayer that they would be kept safe on their journey.

### 

It felt like they had been walking through the forest forever, at least a half hour, and then they noticed a change in elevation. Finn consulted his compass and they made their way south. "Here," he said as he gave Riley the compass, "you keep us going south, I want to do some more EVP recordings. If we do find the caves, and all the legends are true, there may very well be some paranormal activity around here."

Riley continued taking them south when she noticed what looked like an old road. "What in the world?"

"It looks like an old access road," Finn said as they walked from the dense forest onto the old dirt road. He got out his current day map of the terrain to see if he could spot it. "This map I got online obviously isn't zoomed in to where we are, but it should be right about here," he said as he pointed to a spot covered in what looked like broccoli.

"Those satellite images were taken in the summer, full vegetation, you can't even see down here. And if you look further out, there aren't any signs of a road nearby, except all the way over here." Riley pointed to a spot on the opposite side of the hill.

"According to the trail map, that area is all crossed off as treacherous, no trail to hike on, like those areas along the creek that get too rocky and steep to actually hike on." Finn's interest was clearly piqued.

Riley's stomach did a flip. "Someone could still be using this road," she said in a whisper.

"If they have four-wheel drive, they totally could." Finn looked at the steep, rocky, rutted road. "Well, let's follow it." He tied a ribbon nearby, but this time low to the ground so it wasn't as noticeable.

"Is it safe to follow the road? What if someone comes along?" Riley was getting scared. Her imagination could make her scared very easily, especially when she was out in the middle of nowhere.

"Trust me, if someone is coming up this way to conceal dogs, they aren't going to be on foot. They will be in a four-wheel drive vehicle and we'll hear them way before they see us."

Riley took a deep breath. "Okay, let's go."

Finn and Riley followed the road up a steep slope, but then it leveled off and headed back down hill. "This isn't right," Finn said. "What does the compass say?"

Riley looked at the compass, "It looks like the road goes north."

Finn looked at the compass, then up to his left. "I think we need to go back that way, maybe the road doesn't lead to the caves."

"Well, that would make sense, otherwise someone would have found it by now. It's pretty steep and rocky up that way. I agree, we need to go up higher."

They climbed and climbed up the steep slope and came across a rocky ledge. Finn helped Riley onto the ledge which seemed to be coming out of a huge rock wall. As they walked to the south side of the ledge, they saw a small opening, a really small opening, about four feet wide by three feet tall.

"Do you think this is it?" Riley asked Finn.

Finn looked at the crude map drawn well before they were born. "Well, here's Vickery Creek on this side, and then the Chattahoochee down here…I mean, it looks geographically correct, but there's so little detail on this map, it's hard to tell."

"One thing's for sure. No adult is going to be going in and out of that hole." Riley pointed at the small opening.

Finn crouched down and looked around the opening with his flashlight. It was only 3:30 so there was still light outside, but he wanted to look into this small opening to see if it could be the legendary caves. "The earth isn't disturbed around this opening, and there are spiderwebs around it." He said as he cleared the webs away with his hand, then wiped it on his cargo pants. He stuck his head into the opening and shined his flashlight inside. "But it opens up in here. I think this might be it! The dogs may not be kept here, but I think these are the Cherokee Caves, Riley!"

Riley was excited they had found the caves, and a little relieved that they wouldn't be coming across some nasty person who was harming animals, but she really did want to find out what was happening to the dogs and where on earth they were coming from. "Cool!" She paused. "You know I'm claustrophobic, right?"

Finn stood up. "Don't worry, it opens up in there. If you can get past the opening being so small, you'll be fine." Her friend was grinning from ear to ear, but he noticed her disappointment. "Okay, so this may not be where the dogs are being kept, but we found the legendary Cherokee Caves! Let's explore them a bit and do a little ghost hunting. We've got about two hours before we start to lose light." Finn looked at his watch and hoped he could convince his friend to go along with it.

"Okay, but we still need to be careful. If this was where Cherokee gold was hidden, these caves could be booby-trapped," Riley said.

"You're right, but if we found these caves, I'm sure some-one else found them long ago and if there was Cherokee gold in here, I'm sure it's long gone."

"But we still need to be careful. There could be a curse on these caves if there aren't booby-traps.

Finn chuckled, "I love your imagination. We'll be safe, don't worry. I'll go in first and take a look around, make sure there aren't any bears hibernating," he said with a wink.

"Oh great, now you've got me all worried about bears! At least they would be hibernating, right?"

Finn laughed. "See how I took your mind off the boo-by-traps and curses! Be right back!" He hollered as he crawled through the opening into the cave on his belly.

Finn searched the cave with his flashlight. It was surprisingly a fairly open space. No bears hibernating, just a small, rocky chamber. He guessed it was about seven feet tall and about ten feet wide. It was oval in shape, wider than it was deep. He poked his head out of the opening and said, "Coast is clear!"

Riley said a silent prayer, took a deep breath and crawled into the cave. She hated feeling trapped, didn't like small spaces. She was relieved when she got in the cave and found it to be larger than she imagined. "Okay, this isn't so bad." She wiped her hands off on her jeans and smoothed them across her hair to be sure no spiders had tagged along for the ride. She followed the light from Finn's flashlight around the cave.

"I think we found the Cherokee Caves!" Finn lit up the chamber and scanned the walls.

"Cave." Riley corrected him. "This is just one cave, but yes, it is cool." She smiled and looked at her phone. "I texted Eve while you were checking things out and told her we might have found a cave, too small to house any dogs. There's no signal in here, though, of course. I realized we hadn't checked in and I didn't want her worrying."

"Cool, good idea. Hey, let's do an EVP session!"

"Okay!" Riley agreed as they sat across from each other on the rocky dirt floor of the cave. She was glad there weren't any booby-traps in here. Her imagination really could go wild. She was still keeping an ear out for bears, though, or snakes, or raccoons, wild animals in general, this would certainly be a good place to hibernate.

Finn started recording. "Is anyone with us?"

Silence.

"Is this the cave where Cherokee gold was hidden?" Riley asked.

Silence.

"Are there any Cherokee Indians here with us?" Finn asked.

Silence.

"If there's someone here, can you tell us your name?" Riley suddenly felt cold, the hair on her neck and arms was standing up.

Silence.

"We want you to know we mean no harm," Finn said. "We

just want to say hello."

"Did you hear that?" Riley whispered.

"I thought I heard a voice." Both kids were talking as quietly as possible.

"Me too." They both sat still and quiet, waiting. "It sounded like it came from back there." Riley pointed over Finn's right shoulder.

"It did." Finn whispered back. "Let's go over there, all I saw was a pile of rocks." He put his mini recorder in his pocket, leaving it on in hopes that he could capture a spirit communicating with them.

They quietly and slowly headed toward the back right side of the cave and as they got closer, they realized there was a pile of large rocks in front of a narrow passageway. Finn stretched his arm as far as he could, shining his light into the dark corridor.

"I can't see much, but it's definitely a passageway of some kind. Do you want to check it out?" Finn asked Riley who looked nervous about the small space.

Riley tucked her hair behind her ear and said, "I think we should. In case we find the dogs." Her stomach was in knots just thinking of the enclosed space and what they might find.

"Okay, only if you're sure."

"Yeah, I'm good. Let's do this," Riley said as Finn helped her over the rocks and followed behind her.

As they entered the dark passageway, it felt colder and Finn's flashlight started to flicker.

"Great." This made Riley more nervous. "Batteries dead?"

"I just put new ones in. Could be battery drain from a ghost," Finn said with a bit of excitement knowing that spirits often used power sources to obtain energy.

Riley tried her phone to use it's flashlight feature, but it was dead as a hammer. "No luck here, either."

Finn moved in front of Riley, "Let's just move slowly and carefully." No sooner had he said that then Riley squealed and knocked into Finn's back.

"What? What is it?" Finn turned around.

"Something was in my hair, something got in my hair!" Riley danced up and down patting at her head to make sure there was nothing in it.

Finn could hardly see Riley, let alone what might have been in her hair. "Do you feel anything? I can't see..."

"No...," Riley said, when all of a sudden they heard a really high pitched squealing coming toward them and felt the air around their heads fluttering.

"Bats!" Finn yelled and they broke into a run, which seemed like a good idea until they got about eight feet down the tunnel. All of a sudden, they started to fall and tumble. What in the world? Finn thought. While they were falling, the surface was smooth, almost like a slide. Finn hit the bottom, hard, landing right on his backside on a hard, dirt floor. He heard Riley when she hit the bottom, but he must have landed further out than she did, because he couldn't hear her, or see her. It felt much darker in this chamber.

"Riley! Riley! Are you okay?" Finn called out into the darkness. "Riley?" Finn was scared, searching the darkness for his best friend. He saw a light, his flashlight was about four feet from him and was back on. He crawled over and grabbed it, thankful it was working again. He searched the area around him and saw Riley laying flat on her back, motionless. Finn rushed over to her, knelt next to her and felt for a pulse in her neck. Thankfully, there was one.

Finn lightly patted Riley's shoulder and said, "Riley, are you okay?"

She looked up at his worried face and nodded. She tried to speak, but it was difficult. She struggled to say, "Yeah…I'm… fine." She could hardly breathe.

"Shh, just lay there, I think you got the wind knocked out of you." Relief washed over Finn and he knelt by his best friend, unconsciously holding her hand.

Riley squeezed her friend's hand and after a moment quietly said, "I think I'm okay. I want to sit up."

After Finn helped her up, he took a small canteen off his waistband and unscrewed the top. "Here, have some water."

Riley had landed near whatever it was they had slid down and Finn shined his light up it to see if they could go back the way they came.

"It looks like some kind of smooth slide, actually cut into the stone. It's really steep, I don't think we'll make it back up that way," Finn said concerned with how they were going to get out of there. It was cold in this cave and he knew that they weren't dressed for this, not prepared at all. He was so mad at himself. How could I be this careless? He thought.

"I guess we found a booby-trap." Riley's voice was still hoarse, but her sense of humor still intact. She was scared, but knew Finn was as well. They had clearly gotten in over their heads and shouldn't have kept searching.

"Riley, I'm so sorry, I shouldn't have said to keep going. I was so excited about ghost hunting in here, I should have been more careful. We should have left and called Mr. Rycroft."

"Don't apologize, you didn't force me to go with you, I was just as anxious to see if the dogs were being kept in here, and look," she waved her arm out in front of her, "there's nothing here but a small, rocky chamber with low ceilings. Really low ceilings."

"Yeah, I was hoping you wouldn't notice that." Finn's dirt-covered face broke into a grin. He set down his flashlight so it was pointing into the room and fished in his pocket for his compass. He wanted to get his bearings.

Riley picked up the flashlight and started investigating the small chamber. Finn looked up just as his EMF meter went off. "Riley, wait!" Finn yelled, but it was too late.

Riley was shining the light toward the back wall of the chamber and didn't notice what was at her feet, a false floor, camouflaged to blend in with the hard dirt floor they had landed on. Riley fell through, but was able to grab the side of the hole as the flashlight clanged to the bottom where it shattered into pieces. All Riley could tell was that it was a long way down, longer than the slide they just encountered and she knew she couldn't survive that fall.

# CHAPTER TWENTY-FOUR

# *An Unimaginable Discovery*

Finn rushed over to the edge and grabbed Riley's right hand with both of his hands. "Hang on, Ri, please just hang on!"

Riley's grip was slipping and her hands were weak. Finn was praying that he could save his friend, struggling with all his might, his hands hanging tightly to his friend's forearm.

"Please, Ri, just hang on to me!" Finn was terrified what would happen if he couldn't pull her out of the hole. He pulled with all his might and didn't feel like he was even pulling her up an inch. He was silently praying for help.

Finn's EMF meter was going wild in his pocket and all of a sudden, he felt like he had super-human strength. He heaved Riley out of the deep, dark hole in the ground. The two kids fell onto their backs by the edge of the hole, breathless with fright. As soon as he caught his breath, Finn sat up and again, sat over his friend.

"Are you okay, Ri? Are you okay?" He was so scared, he couldn't hide it if he tried, but it was so dark in that cave, he knew Riley couldn't see the fear on his face.

"My arm. It hurts really bad." Riley touched her right arm by the shoulder as she sat up slowly.

"Just take it easy." Finn helped Riley sit up.

"It's so dark. How are we going to get out now?" Riley was terrified and blinked back tears.

"Hang on." Finn searched his pockets yet again. He pulled something out and Riley heard a snap. A green light glowed in front of her.

"A glow stick? What don't you have in those pockets?" Riley was glad she could still find her sense of humor in such a dire situation.

Finn laughed, "A magic wand. That could surely get us out of here."

"Yeah, instead of a magician, I got a Boy Scout." Riley joked.

"When you were heading for the back wall, did you see something over there?"

"Yeah, I thought I saw an alcove, maybe another passageway?"

"Okay, you sit tight, I'm going to check it out." Finn headed slowly to the other side of the chamber using the dim light of his glow stick, careful to avoid the pit in the ground. As he was halfway across the chamber, he stopped in his tracks. "Do you hear that?" He asked Riley in a whisper.

"I hear a voice," Riley whispered back.

"Me, too, and I don't think it's a ghost. I think it's coming from above us." Finn quietly neared the back wall of the tight chamber. As he got to the rear of the chamber, the voice stopped, it was dead quiet again. "Riley, you aren't going to believe this."

"What, what is it?" Riley squinted to see Finn, or at least the green glow from his glow stick.

Finn said as quietly as he could, "There are stairs back here!"

"Stairs?" Riley wasn't sure she had heard her friend correctly.

"Well, kinda stairs. It's like a slope that's terraced." Finn craned his neck and held his glow stick up higher, "it looks well-worn and narrow, but it's worth a try!" He was careful to keep his voice low.

"Awesome! Let's get out of here."

Finn made his way back to his bruised friend, helped her off the ground and guided her over to the small space where the stairs were located.

"I see what you mean, those stairs are kinda primitive and that passage is gonna be tight." Riley knew they would have to shimmy through it to get to a terraced incline.

"Do you want me to investigate first?" Finn asked, seeing Riley was panicked just looking at the tight space she would have to squeeze through.

"No, it's our only choice. We have to go that way, and if there's someone up there, that must be the way out, but I'll let you lead the way." Riley just wanted to get out of there.

Riley and Finn squeezed through the tight passage, they slowly and carefully climbed the narrow, terraced slope upward. They had to use their hands to pull themselves up to each level. It was dark and damp and now that Riley's adrenaline had worn off, she was cold and whispered, "Let's just get out of here in one piece."

As the terraced slope leveled off, there was another tight passage, but this one was different. There was an overpowering smell that struck the kids as soon as they entered. Then they heard the voice again.

"You filthy beasts, you disgust me! If you didn't make me so much money, I wouldn't have anything to do with you. Nasty creatures!" A male voice snarled somewhere in the darkness.

Riley could hear her heart pounding in her ears. She could feel her heart pounding in her chest. Finn grabbed her arm then tucked his glow stick deep into his pocket. It was so dark now, they couldn't see a thing, but they couldn't risk being discovered by the person whose nasty voice they heard, either. Finn felt around them. He could feel the end of the passageway and they must have been headed toward a third cave, though it was so hard to see. They tiptoed forward and heard a growl, then another. Finn and Riley crouched, hidden behind the passage wall and a pile of rocks at its end. They saw a low light flash briefly across the walls, just long enough for them to see that there was another chamber and there was something lining the walls, though they couldn't see what. Whomever was in there had left the chamber. Riley was anxious to get out of these caves, her hands trembled, her heart raced. They waited for several minutes and heard nothing.

Finn whispered to Riley, close to her ear so only she could hear him, "I think I saw another opening, or exit diagonally across from us. Should we try to make a run for it?"

"I saw some large rocks directly across from us, let's make our way there, then wait to make sure he doesn't come back," Riley whispered.

"Okay, let's go!" Finn grabbed Riley's hand and the two kids climbed over the rocks and sprinted to the other side of this much larger chamber. Finn was much quicker and just before he got to the large boulder, he lost Riley's hand, turned and heard what sounded like Riley tripping on something.

Riley skidded across the dirt on her knees and palms.

"Ouch!" She said in a loud whisper.

"Are you alright?" Finn whispered into the darkness. He couldn't see her.

"Yeah, I'm fine." She crawled across the hard dirt on her hands and knees. "Where are you?"

"I'm over here. Follow my voice, I think I'm right in front of you."

Riley was feeling around on the ground when she felt something. It was soft, but firm. Is this fur? She thought as she tried to decipher what this object was. Then came the flash, like a bolt of lightning. It's a dog, it was painfully killed, a blow to the throat. She gasped and clutched her own throat involuntarily.

"Who's there?" Screamed the angry voice. More growls and whimpers this time.

Riley quietly continued in the direction she was going and felt Finn's hand and he pulled her behind the boulder. The growls and whimpers turned in to barking. Loud, anxious barking. Frantic.

A light flashed around the cave walls, again from someone else's flashlight. His flashlight. That's when they saw what was lining the walls. Cages upon cages of sick, malnourished dogs, all covered in filth, hardly recognizable as dogs. Riley's heart dropped to her stomach.

"Must have been one of you nasty beasts making that racket. Shut up! All of you!"

They didn't shut up, though. They were hungry and sick and this horrible excuse for a human being had done this to them. The man set his light down and they heard a shovel hit the ground, scoop something up and put it in a plastic bag.

They heard this three times, the final time, just a few feet from them. Riley was trying to keep her breath quiet, her heart still pounding like crazy. They heard the man pick up the bag and pick up his light, it shined along the cave walls one more time. "If I didn't make so much money off your puppies, you'd all be dead! Filthy beasts." The terrified dogs continued barking frantically, scratching at their chicken wire and rotten wood cages.

The light faded and Riley and Finn were in complete darkness again. Another whimper, this time from Riley. She had tears running down her cheeks.

"Are you okay?" Finn whispered.

"I'm fine." Riley wiped her tears away. "This is horrific. Even with all that I saw, I could never have imagined this. There's no way a normal human being does this. I'm mad. *Really* mad."

"We've got to go after him," Finn whispered. "We need to at least get a look at him and see who he is, then we can tell Mr. Rycroft."

"You're right, let's go."

They carefully and quietly got up and felt their way to the passageway that they presumed would lead them out of the cave. The dogs continued to bark, but not as frantically as before. Riley wished she could open their cages and let them all out right now, but she knew they would need help and care. First they had to catch this nasty man.

Finn and Riley followed the dark passage that the man had come and gone from, it must be the way out. They cautiously made their way toward the light, not worried about booby-traps anymore. They finally made their way to an opening and stayed just inside the cave. As they looked out the large opening, about six feet tall by three feet wide, they saw him, a male figure was standing with his back to them.

Riley gasped and grabbed Finn's arm to steady herself. "That jacket. I know who that is."

"Who?" Finn whispered just as the figured turned so they could see his profile.

It was the profile of Evan Rycroft, and Riley's heart sank.

Finn and Riley looked at each other in disbelief.

"No way!" Finn whispered.

Evan Rycroft had on the leather jacket he had lent Riley when he drove her home after her fall in Vickery Creek. She recognized it immediately. She couldn't believe it. They heard Evan speaking to someone they couldn't see.

As they neared the cave opening they saw a white pick-up truck...and Mr. Rycroft standing near it. He was looking around, and boy did he look angry. He looked up to his left and saw something, or rather someone, "Hey Jedidiah! Have you seen any kids around here?"

Finn and Riley exchanged shocked and confused looks with one another.

"Nope, I ain't seen any kids. Besides, it's late, it's almost dark." It was the angry male voice, the kids couldn't see him, but they could hear him.

Riley was trying to place the name with the voice and it dawned on her.

"My daughter thinks her friends are out here ghost hunting. She hasn't heard back from them in a while and was worried something happened to them," Mr. Rycroft said. "You haven't seen anyone at all?

"Nope. Just getting some work done," Jedidiah said and the kids could hear the nervousness in his voice. He came into view and was carrying a large black plastic bag.

"You okay?" Mr. Rycroft asked, walking toward the truck. "You don't look so good."

"Yeah, I'm fine. I'm gonna be on my way. I'll look out for those kids, let you know if I spot them on my way down." Jedidiah opened his driver side door.

"Mister Rycroft!" Riley sprinted out of the cave toward Detective Rycroft, Evan, and the nasty man named Jedidiah. As Riley got closer, she confirmed who it was–the man from the hardware store, Mister Thornton's caretaker, Jedidiah "Jed" Clinton.

Finn was right on Riley's heels. "That's the man who has been hurting the dogs!

"Whoa, whoa, whoa, kids, slow down. What's this all about?" Mr. Rycroft asked.

"That nasty man, he's got dogs back there in cages and they are all sick!" Riley's heart raced again.

"He's got dead ones in that bag!" Finn pointed to the bag in Jed's hands.

"Jed, what's this all about?" Mr. Rycroft asked.

"Crazy kids with big imaginations, I guess. I'm just clearing trash." Jed looked as nervous as a cat on a glass table.

Finn pulled his recorder out of his pocket, "Here, I was recording while we were in there! I never turned it off."

"Well, if there's nothing but trash in the bag, can I take a look?" Detective Rycroft asked.

Just then, Jed took off running through the woods with

the bag. Detective Rycroft called for back up and looked at Evan. "Take Riley and Finn home then get yourself home. I'll meet you there." He took off running in the direction Jedidiah Clinton was headed.

After running about one-hundred yards as fast as he could, through thickets and woods, Detective Rycroft saw no sign of Jedidiah Clinton. It was quickly growing dark and cold...and it was as if Jedidiah had just disappeared.

# CHAPTER TWENTY-FIVE

## *Life Savers*

The next morning, Riley awoke with a start. Her mom opened her bedroom door and turned on the light. "Rise and shine!"

"Mom, what's going on? What time is it?" Riley could barely open her eyes and the overhead light was blinding, it was still dark outside, but her mom was dressed in jeans and a casual sweater, make-up and hair already done.

"It's six o'clock, time to get up." Her mom was carrying a tray of food.

Riley groaned then winced at the pain in her shoulder, then she remembered…"Did they catch him?" She was now wide awake.

Her dad had just walked in and said, "They sure did, and you'll love who caught him!"

"Who?"

"Jethro, a police dog! Jed thought he knew all the hiding places in those woods, but the dog sniffed him out."

"No way!"

"Yep, poetic justice, huh?"

"That's so cool!" She looked at her mom, breakfast tray still in hand. "Is part of my punishment getting up before sunrise? And if I'm in trouble, why the breakfast in bed?" Riley sat up and propped her pillow against the headboard of her bed, favoring her bum shoulder.

"We've got work to do, so you need your nourishment. Eat up then get ready." Her mom set the tray up over Riley's lap and Riley dug into the food.

"Wear something that you don't mind getting dirty," her dad said as he left the room as well.

Her parents didn't seem mad, but Riley couldn't figure out what was going on. She was starving so she scarfed down the scrambled eggs, bacon, and toast then took a hot shower. Her arm was still really sore and she was scraped up from Finn saving her from the pit in the cave. She thought back to last night and how scary everything was. "I'm really in for a major punishment," she said to her reflection in the mirror as she pulled her hair into a ponytail.

Riley's parents didn't say much as they got in the car and headed out of the neighborhood. Riley was surprised when they turned down Mill Street and the steep hill to Old Mill Park. "What's going on?" She saw the entire area around the park was cordoned off with police tape. There were tents set up in the parking lot, and news vans and police cars were lined up along the sidewalk that led downhill to the parking area.

"It's time to get those dogs out of that cave." Her dad smiled at her in the rear view mirror.

Her mom turned around. "Mr. Rycroft asked if you wanted to be here. It was too late to get the volunteers here last night, so they set-up generators so they could heat the cave and set up lights. Officers stood guard all night."

"Wow, look at all the people." Riley was in awe of the number of people preparing to help the dogs.

"Those tents are where veterinarians will evaluate the dogs," her dad said. "Then they've got folks who will clean them and groom them so they can be comfortable before transport."

Riley realized the enormity of the situation, "How many dogs are there?"

"I think Mr. Rycroft said about 50," her mom said.

Riley's dad parked the car and they got out to be met by Finn and his parents and Eve and her dad.

"Okay, now that we're all here, let's get going," Mr. Rycroft said.

It was still so early that there was a fog over the creek and the morning was cold. Once they got to the trail system, they saw a small fleet of all-terrain vehicles that were being used to take volunteers up and down the trail. When they got to the top, Rhonda was waiting for them by the entrance to the cave. "There they are! Come here you two." Riley and Finn went over to Rhonda who gave them a big bear hug. "You two are brave and you've saved many lives. Next time, tell an adult first though, okay?" Everyone broke into laughter.

"Now, it's pretty rough in there," Mr. Rycroft said, "so if you don't want to go into the cave, we can use your help out here."

Eve and Riley's mom opted to stay outside while Riley, Finn, Mr. & Mrs. Murphy, and Riley's dad offered to go inside and help retrieve the dogs.

Rhonda looked at Riley and Finn, "Are you sure you want to go in there? It's going to be a lot different seeing it lit up… and it's not an easy sight."

"I'm sure," Finn said.

"I have to," Riley said. "I have to see what he did, besides I want to help them." She didn't know if she could handle it, but she felt like she needed to see this through to the end.

"Here, you're going to need these." Rhonda grabbed boxes of surgical gloves and face masks off a portable table. "You're the only kids involved because this is a job for adults, but your parents agreed that if you were comfortable going back in, you could."

Riley's stomach turned. She put on gloves and a mask and followed Rhonda. Finn was by her side, "Are you sure about this?"

"Positive," Riley said. Her dad was on her other side and grabbed her hand; she immediately felt safer.

"This job is a bit bigger than Angels can handle because there are so many dogs," Rhonda said as they headed back to the chamber, "so National Mill Dog Rescue is going to join us in this. They are a national organization dedicated to rescuing dogs from puppy mills. We're glad to have them in to help."

"How many dogs are there?" Riley asked, looking at the entrance cave which looked much different with all the lights set-up. She braced herself as they headed back to the chamber where she knew the dogs were.

"It was a fairly large operation with 43 breeding dogs and some very young puppies that haven't been sold off yet. There are larger mills, but considering this one was done in secret, it was a large operation for an unregulated mill," Rhonda said.

"What do you mean by unregulated? You mean this is legal?" Riley asked.

"In the U.S., any breeder with more than three female breeding dogs who sells to pet stores or brokers must be licensed and inspected. Clearly this one wasn't being monitored. I'm sure it wasn't licensed given it's secret location. Honestly, though, there are so few people to inspect facilities across the U.S., many of the licensed mills don't get the scrutiny they should. There's just not enough manpower," Rhonda said.

"Forty-three dogs!" Finn said. "How are we going to find homes for all of them?"

"Well, that's why we're glad to have the support of National Mill Dog Rescue. Some of the dogs are in pretty bad shape. They have lots of medical issues since they've never seen a vet in their lives. We will triage all of them and are working with local veterinarians on getting them care. Those with the most medical problems will stay here in Georgia since they are too ill to travel and we will nurse them back to health. There are several that are pregnant and we'll likely keep them as well. National Mill Dog Rescue and Angels Among Us are going to take these dogs into our programs. We're actually planning on having an adoption event soon for those that are healthy enough to be adopted out. There are a few that just need a good clean-up, spay, neuter, some vetting, and TLC. The more donations and foster homes we can get, the more dogs we can take in."

As they walked into the chamber where the dogs were kept, Riley heard gasps from everyone. It was hard not to react to such conditions. Just like the night before, the stench hit you before you walked in. There was nothing sanitary about this place. Riley was not prepared for the sight she saw. Some of the dogs didn't look like dogs. They were so matted and filthy you couldn't tell what kind of dog they actually were.

A system was set-up where dogs were taken out of cages

and carried out to be placed in crates and taken down to the parking lot to be evaluated. Rhonda looked at Finn and Riley, "Are you two sure you can handle this?"

They nodded in agreement.

The kids were only handed dogs that showed no aggression and they took their duties very seriously. Riley was afraid what would happen when she touched the dogs, but when she took the first dog, she exhaled in relief, it didn't have anything to say to her. The little dog felt like skin and bones in Riley's hands, she spoke to it and petted it to soothe it. "Shh, it's okay sweet baby, we're going to get you all better." She held back tears as she thought of what this dog had been through, she just didn't understand how anyone could do this. It's fur was matted and filthy.

On her way back in, she saw her dad with an arm full of little black puppies and a smile on his face. Riley was so proud of what they were doing. For just a moment, she thought of what it would be like to adopt one of those puppies.

# CHAPTER TWENTY-SIX

# New Beginnings

On Monday, the school was a-buzz with the news reports of what had happened over the weekend. It seemed everyone was congratulating Riley and Finn, everyone except Corey Thornton and his crew. They were as sour and rude as they ever were.

"Well, we did get his dad's employee in trouble," Finn said as they passed the motley trio in the hallway near the library.

"Why are they always just hanging around?" Eve asked as they headed toward the library.

"I guess they don't have anything better to do." Riley locked eyes with Corey. Was he trying to intimidate her?

"Well, well, well, look who we have here!" Mrs. Willnow barked at Riley, Finn, and Eve as they entered her domain. "My magnificent three! Come here!" She hugged all three of them at once.

"You aren't mad at us?" Riley asked as she got crushed by the hug, wincing as a sharp pain shot through her shoulder.

"Of course I'm mad!" Mrs. Willnow's loud voice boomed, but her eyes twinkled and mouth turned up in a broad grin. "But I'm too proud of you to stay mad at you! I love dogs. They are the best. I'm so glad you caught that jerk."

Riley loved that the librarian with the un-librarian voice was comfortable enough with them to speak her mind. She certainly wasn't the stereotypical librarian. She was loud and full of life. They filled her in on everything. She loved a good story, especially one where the bad guy loses and the good guy wins. Today she let the kids eat their lunches at the back table by her office so she could get all the details. "I hope they lock him up and throw away the key!" She said when she heard about the conditions the dogs were in.

"That's what I said," Riley said as she peeled her banana.

"Listen, you three need to be careful and keep a low profile. You've just gotten Hadrian Thornton's employee in a lot of trouble. For some reason, that man runs this town and I'm sure he's not too happy about what just happened." Mrs. Willnow lowered her voice even though they were the only ones in the library.

"You don't think Mr. Thornton was involved, do you?" Finn asked.

"Oh, no! I don't think he was involved, why would he be? He's rich, powerful, what does he need with selling puppies? No, I just think he's going to be really upset that his estate manager is up a creek."

"My dad works with Mr. Thornton." Riley was suddenly aware that this could be bad for her dad's career.

"Oh, great!" Mrs. Willnow said, back to her loud voice. "Well, honey, you did the right thing and I know your dad, your parents, would take that over anything else. Just you three keep a low profile around Corey and his buddies. I shouldn't be saying this to you, but there's something with that kid, just be careful around him, he's a sneaky one."

"Don't worry, you aren't saying anything we don't already know," Eve said as she tossed her apple core into her bag.

"I know, I'm just supposed to be impartial," Mrs. Willnow added with a wink. "So, I've got some good news and I wanted to share it with you three first."

"Cool! What is it?" Finn's face lit up.

"My friend Nancy works with Angels Among Us and she told me they are taking in a lot of the dogs rescued from the mill."

"We heard they were hoping they had enough donations to take in about half of the dogs. Did they get enough?" Finn asked.

"Yes! In the short time since the news broke, Angels Among Us along with National Mill Dog Rescue put the word out that they wanted to help these dogs and the donations came pouring in from all over the country, the world, even!"

"That's awesome!" Riley's heart was full of joy at this news.

"Even better?" Mrs. Willnow asked. "I'm adopting two of the female Yorkie breeder dogs myself!"

"That's great!" Eve said, all three kids were grinning from ear to ear.

"I'm so excited! I've already got names picked out, Maggie and Nikki. Oh, I can't wait until they are ready to come home with me! Of course they need vet check ups and need to get cleaned up, but I'll keep you posted."

"I can't wait to meet them!" Riley's mind and heart were opening up to the idea of another dog for their family. After seeing the dogs yesterday and listening to Mrs. Willnow talk about them today, she thought this might be the perfect opportunity.

As if reading her mind Finn looked at her and said, "What

do you think? Maybe there's a dog for your family from the mill, too?"

"I think there may be. I think I'll talk to my parents tonight and then maybe Rhonda can help us out."

"Just think, we helped save these dogs, it would be very meaningful if your family were to adopt one, if you're all ready for that," Finn said as the bell rang signaling the end of lunch period.

"Thanks for letting us eat in here today," Riley said as she pushed in her chair. "It was fun!"

"Just don't tell anyone." Mrs. Willnow was grinning mischievously. "I can't let the other kids think I'm soft."

"Your secret is safe with us," Finn said as the three headed to the library's exit.

### 

The remainder of the day flew by because everyone in every class wanted to hear about Finn's and Riley's adventure. For two kids who pretty much flew under the radar, this was a unique day at school.

On the way home from school, Riley and Finn were telling each other about the reactions they got in their classes.

"Like your mom said, it was a good opportunity to educate people about puppy mills," Riley said. "A lot of kids didn't realize where pet store puppies come from or how their parents are treated. Hopefully we're making a difference."

"Yeah, I hope so, too. We definitely need to capitalize on this and educate the community, reach out to officials who can strengthen the laws and get pet stores banned in our city, or county."

"I agree. Eve and I were talking about that as well. We should get together this weekend and strategize. Here, I want to show you something." Riley slipped her backpack off and pulled a sheet of paper out of a folder and handed it to Finn. "I designed this and thought maybe we could make t-shirts and stickers."

Finn looked at the image that read, Mill Cotton, Not Puppies. There was an image of a cotton plant and a two puppies. Finn loved it. "This is awesome!"

"You think so?"

"I do, it's great!"

"I figure it has a lot of meaning since the puppy mill was near an old cotton mill. We could sell them and donate a portion of the profits to charities, like Angels Among Us and National Mill Dog Rescue."

"That's an awesome idea, you're really creative, you know."

"Thanks, I'm glad you like it," Riley said as Finn handed the design back to her and she carefully placed it back in the folder.

"Look." Finn stopped and pointed to a white piece of paper taped to a stop sign. "Lost dog."

"Oh no." Riley stepped closer to get a better look. "Looks like a beagle." She snapped a picture with her phone. "That's the second 'Lost Dog' poster I've seen in a week."

"I hate seeing lost dog signs," Finn said.

"I know, I can't even imagine how hard that must be. I don't think I'd sleep if I had a dog that went missing."

"Well, looks like we have a new project," Finn said. "We'll

have to be on the lookout for that little guy."

"Absolutely," Riley agreed as she put her phone in her back pocket and they continued down the sidewalk. "Hopefully it won't end as dramatically as the found dog scenario," she said with a smile.

"Yeah, I think we could use a little down time," Finn said. "We've had enough adventure for a while."

### 

At dinner Monday night, Riley filled her parents and sister in on the reactions they got at school. She was so proud of what they had done that she'd forgotten all about getting punished for doing something that could have gotten her hurt badly, or worse. It was Hailey who reminded her parents upon hearing about her sister's great day at school. "If I did something that stupid, you'd ground me. Aren't you going to punish Riley?"

Riley's heart sped up. Why was her sister doing this to her? Couldn't she be happy that Riley had achieved something great, or was Hailey the only one who could get accolades around this household? She looked at her parents who exchanged glances with one another. Just as her dad was about to say something, her mom set down her silverware and gave Hailey a look that would frighten a grown man.

"Hailey, it is up to your father and me to decide what, if any, punishment your sister will receive. While she did something dangerous, she didn't set out to get herself in that situation and she realizes that she shouldn't have been so careless. If you are done eating, you may take your dishes to the kitchen and be excused." Now their mom looked at Riley. "Riley, when you are finished eating, clean up your dishes and come into your father's office."

Riley's stomach was in knots. Hailey made her so mad and she was pleasantly surprised that her mom stood up for her and put perfect Hailey in her place. However, she wasn't sure she was looking forward to going into her dad's office to find out what her parents thought would be an appropriate punishment.

Hailey smirked at Riley and sauntered into the kitchen with her dishes. Riley was a slow eater and glad for it. She didn't want to go into the kitchen with Hailey because she knew a fight would ensue. She slowly ate the rest of her mashed potatoes and corn, finishing up when she heard her sister go upstairs. After she cleaned up, Riley went into the office where her dad was seated behind his desk, and her mom in one of the two wing-back chairs by the fireplace. Riley sat in the other chair and tucked her hair behind her ear, waiting to hear what her parents had to say.

Her dad broke the silence. "Roo, you know what you and Finn did was dangerous, you really could have gotten hurt."

Riley's mom looked at her, her eyes glossy. "Honey, we were so scared when we found out where you were, what you and Finn had done."

"I'm sorry." Riley looked at the wood floor and the patterns in the area rug. "I was really scared. We knew we should have left and called Mr. Rycroft, but then we were in over our heads. I'm really sorry."

"We know you are, Roo," her dad said as he rested his

elbows on his desk and leaned toward his daughter. "But, it wouldn't be fair if we didn't punish you. You are to do all the dishes after dinner starting tonight, for one month. No help from Hailey, your mom, or me. Any time you want to go somewhere, you let us know. No going off on adventures without letting us know where you are going and with whom you are going. We've been lenient with you because we trust you and your judgment, but after this experience, you have to prove to us that you will make better decisions."

"Yes, sir," Riley said as she looked up at her dad. She thought her punishment could have been much worse and was expecting to be grounded.

As if she had read her mind, her mom said, "We would have grounded you, but you did a really good thing. We're really proud of you."

That was it. Riley lost it and flung herself into her mom's arms, crying. "Thanks, mom. I'm so sorry. I really am."

Riley's mom stroked her daughter's hair. "Oh, honey, it's okay. Shh…"

Riley hugged her mom tightly and looked up as her dad knelt by the chair. She blinked more tears out of her eyes and said, "Thank you for being proud of me." Now it was both of her parents hugging her.

"We're always proud of you, Roo," her dad said as he brushed a tear off her cheek. "We also have an important question for you. Your mom and I were talking last night and well, we thought maybe we would see if we could foster one of the dogs from the puppy mill. We don't have to adopt a dog, especially if you're still not ready, but we think we can help out here." He looked at his daughter, hoping she was ready for this.

Riley's face brightened into a grin and she laughed. Her parents looked at each other, confused. "I was just telling Finn today that I might be ready for a dog, that maybe we could adopt one of the mill dogs!"

Her parents looked relieved and excited. Her dad got up and went back behind his desk, put the phone on speaker and dialed.

"This is Rhonda," the voice said through the speaker.

"Hey Rhonda, Jack Carson calling with Priscilla and Riley. How are you?"

"Great, thanks. How are you?"

"Wonderful, actually. We were thinking, any chance you think one of the mill dogs that's ready for a home would be right for us?"

"It's funny you mention it, because I had that thought today. I couldn't think of a more fitting family for one of these dogs than yours. There are a couple of Maltese, a Bichon Frise, and possibly a Yorkie that might make a great fit for your family, and of course some puppies. The dogs need serious training since they've spent their entire lives in cages, but I know you've got a daughter who would be pretty dedicated to training. As long as the entire family is committed and patient, I think this would work well."

Riley beamed with pride. She felt honored that Rhonda knew she would be able to work with one of these dogs, to train it to live with their family. She was finally excited about the prospect of getting another dog. She knew Sammy would approve.

Riley Carson will return in book two of this series! To stay up to date with news, events, or to join the mailing list, visit:

**www.RileyCarsonSeries.com**


To learn more about Angels Among Us Pet Rescue, visit:
www.AngelsRescue.org

To learn more about National Mill Dog Rescue, visit:
www.MillDogRescue.org

To order your own "Mill Cotton Not Puppies" t-shirt, visit:
www.RileyCarsonSeries.com

# ACKNOWLEDGMENTS

To God for your blessings and showing me this path. Michael, for your constant support and encouragement. Thank you for putting up with me obsessing over the title graphic (and basically every element of this book), for listening to the book read aloud, and for making me dinner every night.

My parents, Mary and Dan Wargula, for giving me so much...always. Thank you for your love, support, and generosity. I hope I've made you proud. My sister, Courtney, for always being there for me and picking out the best birthday cards. Reena Nichols, for encouraging me from the start and following me through to the finish. Your enthusiasm and support mean so much to me. Rhonda Hofer, thank you for teaching me so much about rescue and holding me accountable. Nan Willnow, your zest for life, passion for your work, and loyalty to your friends have forever impacted me. I hope you are watching from heaven and enjoying this journey with me. Tim Harrington, you devilish, supportive, compassionate soul. You are missed and I hope you are enjoying this from heaven, too! Andy Suggs, the most loyal friend and design guru, I appreciate you so much! Denine Attride, my sister from another mother, I love you! Joy Southerland, thank you for your proofreading skills and support! Jim and Lucy for being such wonderful people and fantastic role models. Ellen Tate for blessing me with two amazing border terriers who have changed my life.

To my young beta readers: Aubrey S., Ava B., & Addie S. Thank you for reading my story and giving me valuable feedback. I am forever grateful to your parents for raising such caring, compassionate children.

To other authors who have generously shared their wisdom with me: Raymond L. Atkins, Lee Gimenez, Tianna Holley, Sue Horner, Shelley Pickens, and Jason VanGumster. Kimberly Martin at Jera Publishing for your guidance and resources.

The Roswell Historical Society, The City of Roswell, and Historic Roswell Visitors Center for preserving the history of such a beautiful town. David Wood from Public House for sharing your restaurant and haunted stories with me. Dianna & Joe Avena (and all your tour guides) for keeping the ghost stories and history of Roswell alive via the Roswell Ghost Tour. Table & Main for serving the best fried chicken and for such a warm, welcoming restaurant.

Victoria Stilwell, for teaching me about positive reinforcement dog training, it's the only way! Angels Among Us Pet Rescue and National Mill Dog Rescue for doing work that is heart-breaking, yet rewarding. You are special people and I am grateful for the work you do. Thank you for allowing me to use your names so that we can make a difference for animals together! Luann Farrell and Jeff & Mary Howard, your assistance in working with AAUPR, your support, and enthusiasm mean the world to me. National Mill Dog Rescue and Theresa Strader, I will always be inspired by Theresa and Lily and what one woman with a big heart on a mission can do.

# ABOUT THE AUTHOR

Michael Duisenberg

Megan Wargula is a self-proclaimed "dog nerd" - the kind of person who knows the dogs in her neighborhood better than their humans! A native of Atlanta, Georgia, Megan has always loved animals and has made it her mission to make the world a better place for dogs through her writing. When not at her day job as a graphic designer, Megan spends the rest of her time writing and enjoying life with her husband and dogs, Finlay and Riley. Megan is a fan of history and the paranormal which is part of the reason she loves the town of Roswell, Georgia so much. Many of the places in the book are real, so plan your visit!

Fun Facts: Megan, Finlay, and Riley were fortunate enough to get some training from Victoria Stilwell when she won a contest that included a piece in Oprah Magazine! Oh, and she invited a rock star to her prom back in the 90's and he said yes. She thinks it might have been the very first prom-posal, and is forever grateful to Evan Dando of Lemonheads for being such a nice guy.